ESCAPE TO TEXAS
Twin Creeks Texas Series

Copyright © 2020 Cathy O'Bryan

All rights reserved. Except for use in any review, the reproduction or utilization of this work in whole or in part in any form by any electronic, mechanical or other means, now known or hereinafter invented, including xerography, photocopying and recording, or in any information storage or retrieval system, is forbidden without the written permission of the publisher.

This is a work of fiction. Names, characters, places and incidents are either the product of the author's imagination or are used fictitiously, and any resemblance to actual persons, living or dead, business establishments, events or locales is entirely coincidental.

Printed in the USA.

Cover Design by The Killion Group, Inc.

Escape to Texas

CATHY O'BRYAN

DEDICATION

This novel is a direct result of three wonderful authors, Robin B sweet, Krista Lynne, and Ware Woodson. A big thank you to all of you, but It just doesn't seem enough. My family and friends have always been there for me and I love them for it. Thank you everyone.

ONE

✱

"IF WHAT YOU DID YESTERDAY still looks big, you haven't done much," kept replaying over and over in Sandy's head. Her dad reminded her of those words when she needed them. Today, she needed them. She was glad to have his words in her head.

This drive from Austin through the hill country and beyond was what Sandy needed. This new adventure was a plan devised by her Dad and Bob to keep her safe. The Texas countryside was so different than the roads and small towns back east. Maryland's country roads were usually two lanes that snake around the nooks and crannies of the foothills of the Appalachians. Texas roads were fairly straight and flat as you climb northwest out of Austin. And yes, many times you could see forever. Sandy knew buying a piece of property was a big deal but buying one you have never seen was scary. Bob, dad's best friend, orchestrated the deal, and her dad agreed that this was the perfect solution. The big cities and east coast were far behind and so far in Texas, no one knew who she was. Open doors and wide-open spaces were what the Lone Star

State was known for, right? All the license plates say "The friendly state" and so far, so good.

The old hotel should be the perfect bed and breakfast in this small West Texas town of Twin Creeks. It wasn't too far from Dinosaur Valley State Park, Squaw Creek Reservoir and the Wheeler Branch Reservoir. Sandy was ready to remodel and begin anew.

Bob had sent photos and it seemed that repairs would be needed, but nothing major. Just a little love and TLC. He left the keys and paperwork with Martha, the owner of Martha's Café in the town square. The hotel sits in one corner of the square in the center of town. The library is directly beside the old hotel with an alley in between them. How cool was it to have a library so close? Sandy loved going to the library, especially on rainy or cooler days. The internet can be a great source of research for the DIY and home articles she writes for some magazines, but sometimes the pleasure of thumbing through a book just makes all that researching better.

As Sandy cruises along Highway 281, she found herself singing along with an old western song on the radio that her dad loved, On the Wings of a Snow White Dove Here. It was recorded by lots of artists, like Dolly Parton and Loretta Lynn, but dad liked the Ferlin Husky version. Sandy didn't even know who Ferlin Husky was, but she knew the words and would have recognized his voice anywhere, thanks to her dad. It was her comfort song. She could feel her dad riding along with her.

As Sandy started down from a rise in the road, she could see a small town in the distance. There were small houses set back off the road. Along the fence lines were gardens, swing sets, cattle, and a few goats.

As she got closer, she could see that this little place had that old, Texas charm feel to it. Just ahead she could read the road sign; Hico - two miles. Maybe it's time for a stop to do a little exploring, a bio break and refresh her drink.

According to the GPS, she was a little less than an hour away from Twin Creeks. The solitude of the straight road and lack of other cars had Sandy's mind taking her back to the investigation and what she needed to escape from. The demons were still right there in her head. The radio was now blaring Taylor Swift's Shake it Off and that was exactly what she planned to do. It was high time she left the skeletons behind. No one would look for her in Twin Creeks, or at least she hoped not. Dad and Uncle Bob were sure Pete and "the family" didn't have a clue where she was.

The cute little town of Hico was a mixture of old and new, from an old Dairy Queen to a new Whataburger. Uncle Bob said that there was a café where 281 dead ends into 220. He said The Koffee Kup had the best pies and that she should stop and at least have pie, if not lunch too. It's time to sample some true small-town cooking. Pulling into a crowed parking lot, it was evident that this little café was busy. She could see breakfast and lunch was being served, which usually meant almost everything was cooked to order. The friendly waitress that seated her looked a little surprised she was alone, but took her to a window seat table set for two. Sandy looked around and didn't see any single diners. This was clearly a family-oriented place.

Out the window, she could see the bustle of this little town. Back in D.C., this would be labeled as a sleepy little town, but she could see the quiet movement of its people.

Lunch and a huge piece of pie later, Sandy settled in for the last part of her journey. The lunch was so good, this would be a must-have stop in the future. The coconut cream pie was to die for. If Sandy thought she would have a place to refrigerate a whole pie, one would have traveled with her to Twin Creeks. For now, it would be a pleasant sweet memory with a future visit on her to-do list.

The new Jeep was full of her possessions that Sandy couldn't survive without. The rest was being shipped to Uncle Bob's first, so no one on the other end could find her. Dad and Bob had decided to err on the side of caution and have any trail end in Austin. Sandy's Jeep wasn't even in her name. Bob had it titled in his and his son's name.

The turn on to 56 was Sandy's next milestone. She drives through Glen Rose, a lovely little town that boasts a little over twenty-four hundred people, according to the sign. The courthouse in the square looks like a stately mansion from times gone by. Sandy was tempted to stop and look in all the shops that line the streets around the courthouse, but she had a bigger desire to see her new home in Twin Creeks. This little town needed exploring but at a later date.

Passing through small towns in Texas could be dangerous... well, to your driving record at least. The speed traps were numerous. Twin Creeks was no different, but Sandy was well-practiced after her back-road trek from Austin. She easily spotted the unmarked car nestled in the trees just as the speed limit changes from 70, to 45 and then, within a block, to 35. "You missed me this time," she said to no one in particular, and waved to the officer. To her surprise, he waved back. Crap, should that worry her?

Seconds later, she was in the square, and there was the café. Could there be more than one? Surely not in this small town. Sandy parked and found a bench near the courthouse front door to sit and just take the place in. You know, just to get a feeling of the place... its vibe. She knew there was a bakery somewhere close but she didn't need her eyes to find it. The heavenly smells that wafted toward her from it were enticing. Sandy could see the post office and bank, a tea room, pharmacy, bridal shop, antique shop, hair salon, and then the café all from her seat. They all framed this square with its lovely little park, complete with a gazebo in the middle perfect for a summer dance. The courthouse sat at the head of this imaginary table with the others finishing a charming square. There were also booths lined along the edges that felt like pictures she had seen for an old-fashioned county fair. So pleasant to just sit and take it in. Here goes nothing. It's time to join this small town.

The café was dead quiet, but it was two in the afternoon. The pleasant woman behind the counter was a welcome sight. Sandy tried her friendliest smile, "Hi, I'm Sandy." Vanessa flashed a smile, wiping her hands on her apron. "Been expecting you. Martha was sorry she couldn't meet you herself, but it's been a busy weekend." She motioned toward the square.

"The winter festival kicked off this weekend. Let me get you those keys..." Her voice echoed a bit as she disappeared behind a swinging door, "the realtor from Glen Rose asked me to clean one of the rooms on the first floor so you could spend your first night in your new place." She was still talking when she appeared again.

Vanessa jangled the keys as she came back into the dining room. "It may look shabby, but everything works. The hotel reopening is all anyone's been talking about this weekend. I've heard the Grand McCormick Hotel was the place to stay and a destination in its day. It isn't so grand anymore, but it's still quite lovely."

Vanessa held the keys out, "this key works the front and back doors, but I'd change it if I were you." A flicker of a shadow crossed her face, before she smiled a bit overly bright and continued, "I'd walk over with you but I'm the only person here right now, and Lord but I've babbled enough. Sorry about that." Just as Sandy started to speak, Vanessa started again.

"Oh, the room to the right as you leave the

kitchen is the room I cleaned for you as well as the bathroom and the kitchen, of course. I'm sure you'll want to deep clean and move things but for now, it's clean enough for a few days."

Sandy turned and smiled, "thank you for taking care of things, I'm sure you made it perfect. Can you point me in the right direction so I can unpack a few things? I'll be back later for dinner and to ask questions, if you're open."

Vanessa nodded and moved to the door. As Vanessa and Sandy stepped out onto the porch, Vanessa hunched over a little to point past the trees in the park and down the street, just behind the two biggest oak trees and across to a beautiful building, a cross between a Victorian style and an old western saloon that sported a big porch with turrets and the like. Yes, this could have been the destination back in the day. After a big hug and another heartfelt "thank you," Sandy was off to her new place and next stop on her journey.

As Sandy approached her Victorian/Western beauty, she felt like this could be home. It towers a mere four stories but in this town, it felt more like twenty. Sandy stopped and said a small prayer before she put the key in the door. The key felt right as she turned the doorknob and stepped inside. She closed the door behind herself and the first thing that caught her eye was the check-in desk. It was charming... amazing... no, perfect. The dark-stained oak was stunning, but the elaborate hand-carved parts were a sight to behold. Someone had spent hours creating such a custom piece. Bob was right, this was a treasure that needed restoring and Sandy knew she was up for the challenge.

"Are you Sandy McAllister?" A deep voice coming from behind made her jump and turn, all at once ready to kick butt if needed. He must have sensed her readiness to pounce because his hands went up and he said, "Whoa there, little lady. I'm Dylan Matthews, sheriff here in Twin Creeks. I was told you'd be arriving today, so I'm just making sure everything's ok."

"Yes, I'm Sandy. You scared me." Sandy took a deep breath and extended her hand.

"Yep, I figured that out right away. Sorry about that. Just a few things you should know. The real estate guy will be here in the morning, but the electricity is on and so is the water, so staying here tonight is okay. I'll check on you this evening during my regular rounds. Welcome to Twin Creeks."

Sandy thanked him and he was gone, leaving her to explore this grand old place alone. The first floor had a kitchen, entry hall, sitting area, library with tables, a dining room, a tiny powder room, and three bedrooms with a bathroom between them. One of the rooms was freshly cleaned, and so was the bathroom. Sandy strolled back through first floor, checking out the big kitchen.

The second floor had eight rooms and two bathrooms. Two of the rooms would only allow a small twin bed and nothing else. These would have to be reconfigured, all of it looks dusty but still in working order. So far, Uncle Bob's ability to see a diamond in the rough was ringing true. The third floor housed six rooms and two bathrooms, again in the same grimy but functioning condition.

The fourth floor brought a big surprise with one big, open area and a large enough bathroom to be perfect for her home. She could make this work without too much effort. This fourth-floor gem would only take a few days of work if she could get all the supplies. She wondered how close a home improvement store was. Getting supplies might be the hardest part way out here in the middle of nowhere.

After moving her Jeep to be just outside the front door, and several trips back and forth, Sandy was all moved in for the moment. Time for that trip back to the café and some dinner, then maybe a sit on her lovely, new porch. The cool evening was a nice surprise. It wasn't too cold, but chilly enough for hot chocolate later, if she had some.

Six in the evening found the café busier than before. Seated in the restaurant were five people, and another two more followed Sandy in. Vanessa welcomed Sandy again and introduced her to Martha, the owner of the café. Martha then introduced Sandy to everyone else at once. "Hey everybody… This here is Sandy, the new owner of the Grand McCormick."

Everyone turned to look with smiles on their faces and then they clapped. Sandy felt like a kid in school who had just gotten an A on the spelling test. She nodded and then felt silly. Martha doesn't even notice her discomfort and continued as she walked over to a table full of five men who could all grace the cover of any magazine. Her loving voice began as she placed her hand on one of the men's shoulders, "this here is Mike Stone, the youngest brother of this brood and the deputy sheriff of Twin Creeks." Sandy was amazed that these were all brothers. Martha moved to the next man, "you already met Dylan Matthews, the sheriff. He's a wannabe brother of this crew. Next to him is Liam Stone, he likes to dig in the dirt. I think he calls himself an archeologist. This cutie is Nathaniel Stone and he claims to be a civil engineer. Whatever that is. And then there is Owen Stone, the oldest of this clan of brothers. He's our resident Texas Ranger." Martha had moved around the table as she introduced this brood, as she called them.

Sandy stood still taking in this amazing collection of male physique. The men all cut their eyes at Martha and did their best to smile at her description of themselves. Sandy blushed, either from being the center of attention or from the delicious eye candy sizing her up.

Martha wasn't finished with her introductions. She turned to the two people at the small table by the door; the two who had followed Sandy in, "those two over there are Anna and Jeffery, our sweet little love birds. Hey, take a minute and wave at our new neighbor." They do and Sandy finally made her way back to the counter with Martha. This would be the right time to visit with Martha and learn about this lovely café.

Sandy sat at the counter and picked up the menu. "Martha, tell me about your place. It seems like there's history to be told here." Martha leaned back with a sweet smile and began her story. "Well, the day I got married, my magnificent new husband carried me across the threshold of this place. He wanted me to bake pecan pies here. We lived upstairs in the apartment that Vanessa has now. It was empty for a while cause a few years back we bought a cute little one-story cottage at the edge of a pecan grove. Seemed like God wanted me to be close to them beautiful pecans because I make dang good pecan pies. This place was my wedding gift."

Sandy loved this love story and hoped someday she would tell her own love story. "Martha, that is so sweet. He must love you so much to live your dream with you."

Martha expression went distant them came back to the present. "He was a sweet and loving man, and we were so much in love. I lost him two years ago and without this café, I would have been lost. I see his touch on this place everywhere. This place keeps me grounded."

Sandy regrets touching on such a sad topic and that apparently shows on her face because Martha places her hand over Sandy's. "I love talking about him. I miss him. But it's good for me to share his life and love with others. Thank you for listening."

Sandy smiles shyly. "I will always listen."

Martha pats Sandy's hand again and picks up her order pad. "So, what can I get you tonight?"

Sandy quickly decides to try the special, allowing Martha to retreat and gather her emotions. The evening special, as she had learned from Bob, is a Texas standard on most country menus. Country fried steak, mashed potatoes, and green beans sounded perfect.

Martha stopped to check on her food and asked, "was everything okay at the hotel? I mean, was it cleaned okay?"

"It's perfection! Better than I expected. Who do I owe for the work?" Sandy widened her eyes for emphasis.

Martha's friendly smile grew bigger. "That real estate agent from Glen Rose took care of all that. I put a few things in the fridge for you, too."

Such small-town hospitality. "Why, that was so nice. I haven't even opened the fridge yet. Speaking of goods, where are the closest grocery and hardware stores?" Martha got a pen and paper out and proceeded to draw a map for Sandy. Maybe she wasn't big into GPS just yet.

"We have a small grocery store here, but there's a Walmart in Glen Rose." She was pointing to her hastily drawn map. "You'll also find a new HEB and a Home Depot on the other side of the square of Glen Rose. I believe you can find almost anything you might want in those three. The real estate guy said you might need a handyman, too. I took the liberty of calling Fred Wilson. He'll be here tomorrow evening to see you, about six. That okay?"

"That'd be amazing!" Sandy stammered in disbelief. Sandy pulled out her phone and snapped a picture of Martha's little map, paid her bill, and excused herself for her walk back across the small park to her new place.

This had been a long day and it felt like midnight, even though it was just eight o'clock and just turning dark outside. Time to go home. What a nice sound, "home" in a nice, safe place, she hoped. When Sandy walked over to the café, it was just sunset with hints of a clear crisp evening to come. Now with full darkness, she could see a million stars in the sky.

Once back in her new home, Sandy found instant cocoa and made a cup, then drug a chair to the porch with a blanket to sit for a spell and just breathe it all in.

"The stars at night, are big and bright," so the song goes. Boy, they were both big and bright here tonight. It was so quiet. Every now and again, she could hear and see people come and go from the side door of the café. They were laughing and talking loudly, so it must be fun whatever it was. She noted to herself to remember to ask.

The pretty Christmas decorations the town had on the street lamps didn't interfere with the beautiful starry sky. They added to the charm of this little town. The peaceful street and the light breeze of intoxicating fresh air had Sandy yawning on short order.

After all of the trouble and dangerous times she had left behind, Sandy took her time checking all the doors and windows. Just as she was about to turn the lobby lights out, there was a knock on the front door. It was easy to see the cowboy hat through the etched antique grand door glass. As she approached, the hat's owner spoke. "Dylan Matthews here, just checking on you. No need to open the door unless you want."

With a smile on her face, Sandy opened the door to the beautiful, no gorgeous, cowboy with a badge. "Thank you for your kindness and concern. I think I'm going to enjoy this small town."

He tips his hat at her gratitude. "All's well then, I take it?"

"Yes, I'm just heading to bed. Was that you by the side of the road this afternoon who waved at me as I drove in?"

"Do you mean the speed trap?" he replies.

She nodded. "Yes sir. Just where the speed changes."

"Nope, not me. That was Mikey. I'll be there tomorrow."

With that warning, he stepped back and tipped his hat again. "Night, new neighbor."

Sandy smiled, "thanks again, and a good night to you, too."

A few minutes later, Sandy was in a nightshirt and climbing into bed. This had been a busy Monday and Tuesday would be filled with shopping in Glen Rose. This bed was too nice to have been here too long. Sure enough, on the bedside table was a receipt for a mattress and linens. As Sandy relaxed into bed, she felt grateful for Uncle Bob and her dad and all they had done for her.

Falling asleep lately was difficult for Sandy, but not tonight. Sandy was asleep before her head hit the pillow. If you had asked her, she would have told you that she was worried that the creaks and squeaks of this old place would keep her awake and listening to the noises. She was sure that it would keep her up, but not this night or many more to come.

TWO

THE SUN WAS UP AND so was Sandy. It felt like she had slept forever. She was out of bed, in the shower and dressed before she had the sense to check the time. Holy cow, it was just barely seven-thirty! She hadn't seen seven-thirty in forever, but she was ready for the day.

She headed to the kitchen to see what had been left. Martha was an angel. She had left cinnamon rolls, prepped and ready to slip into the oven. They smelled so delicious. Martha also left coffee, but Sandy was a tea drinker so she found her stash of her favorite tea from her bag and heated water for her morning hot tea ritual. Such a luxury. Her kitchen table was a glow in this bright sun filled room… she was alone but she wasn't lonely.

Sandy sinks her teeth into a fluffy, fragrant roll and immediately decides she must know where Martha gets the cinnamon rolls. They were addicting, and it was going to be a challenge to only have one and save the rest for later. It was beautiful outside and she quickly decided she'd add in a short run around town square.

With the front door locked, the key tucked in a pocket of her jacket and her phone in the other, Sandy headed out. Her run would be short and slow today. Since she hadn't been able to do this in a while, her muscles would need a slow warm-up. Jogging in place, she went right from the front porch and headed toward the far side of the square to circle the small park, Foster Park according to the sign. There were cars in the parking lot and people coming and going. Busy place for the Monday after Thanksgiving. Many waved and smiled like she was their long-lost sister. It was nice to feel wanted and welcomed. As she crossed the street and turned for home, Sandy remembered that there was a festival in town.

As she approached the hotel, she saw a man unloading boxes in the alley. She slowed to watch which way he was going with such a heavy looking box in his arms. He looked to be about her age, maybe a little older, and definitely cute. He leaned up against the back door to the library, fished out a key and unlocked the door, and disappeared inside. A few seconds, later he was out and locked the door behind him. As she approached in her slow jog, he looks up and waves. She waves back at him and he disappears inside the building she had been told was the library. Her curiosity piqued, she rounds the corner of the library and jogs up to the front door. Putting both hands on the door window, she peers through the glass, but the window was tinted so no luck. Before she could step back, the door opens and she falls in. Sandy doesn't hit the floor but rather finds herself in the arms of the same, nice smelling, strong man from the alley.

Sputtering, she said, "I am so sorry. Is this the library and are you open?" Dang, he was nice to look at.

With a chuckle, strong hands stood Sandy up. "Yep, that's what the sign says. Somervell County Library Annex. Hours are 8 to 5, Monday, Wednesday and Friday, and Saturday, 8 to noon. Are you the new owner of the hotel and my neighbor?"

He takes a step back and looks her up and down. "Liam said you were a looker and he was right. He likes anything in a skirt, so I wasn't sure. Sorry, no offense. Welcome to the neighborhood."

Sandy was not so direct with people so this man had made her stop dead with his unfiltered comments. "Thanks, I think. Yes, I'm Sandy McAllister, your neighbor. Do you work here?"

"Yes, I'm the librarian here at LA, short for Library Annex. The Somervell County Library is in Glen Rose, this is just the annex."

Even though this man was defiantly eye candy and Sandy liked his straightforward manner, she had an alarm going off in her head. She felt nervous and kind of sht. Sandy had never been described as shy, and nervous of what? As he moved in closer, she felt warm and uncomfortable, but she wasn't afraid. What was it about him?

"Hey, I have coffee brewing. Want some?"

She was dragged back to the present and out of her inner thoughts. Startled by his voice, she stammered out, "I have a million errands to run. I'm heading out to Glen Rose for some supplies, but I'll take a rain check."

Sandy started to turn and back away when he reached out and touched her arm. With just that gentle touch, a lovely jolt of electricity rang through her. Did he feel that too, or was it just her? As she looked up into his eyes, she could see he felt something, too. Sandy was frozen, so hopefully he couldn't tell. It had been a long time since she had an instant connection. The last time that had happened, she got connected to the wrong man. Ok, according to her lady parts, he was the right man, just from the wrong family. Even in her head that sounded wrong. The lesson here was 'don't trust yourself just yet.'

Pete had been a lovely Italian stallion and boy, could he ever kiss. But when you took a moment and looked past him to his family and friends, well, you couldn't miss that there was a big problem hidden just out of sight. Thinking about his close connection to the mob made Sandy shiver. The man in front of her felt her shiver and looked deeper into her eyes. It was hypnotizing.

This beautiful man was nothing like Pete. Shoving those scary memories aside, Sandy pulls her wits back to the present. "I, uh... I don't think I got your name."

He seems to be lost in his thoughts, too, "I... uh...I'm Jonathan Wells. I live in Glen Rose for now and work here part-time. I'm also a published writer of murder mysteries and I write a local column for The Twin Creeks Tribune. It's about book reviews, recommendations, seasonal reading lists and contests. Okay, that may have been way too much information in one sentence. Just call me Jon and I will hold you to the coffee time together. It's very quiet here most days, so I always have time for coffee. Damn, there I go rambling again. We can talk later."

As he finished his lengthy introduction, his hand had lingered on Sandy's arm and then as if snake struck him, he removed it. Sandy had forgotten his hand was there. It felt comfortable, no, natural.

Sandy smiled and started jogging in place ready to continue her new routine. "Thanks Jonathan. I mean Jon. I'll come by soon for the coffee." To her retreating back he shouts, "Make it soon."

Sandy waved and was gone around the corner. As she stepped back onto the porch of the hotel, she looked around. For what, she wasn't sure, maybe just habit. There were only a few people out and no one was even looking her way. It would take a while to get used to this safe place. Time to check out the stores in Glen Rose.

Glen Rose did have a Home Depot and it was Sandy's first stop. Today, she would just get a few immediate things for her new place on the top floor. Getting started on that was all about her comfort. A coat of paint and cleaning supplies for the floor, now those two things were a good place to start. After picking up floor cleaner and some other simple cleaning tools, Sandy headed over to look at paint. Her bedding that was arriving tomorrow with the rest of her furniture were shades of blues and purples. Sandy picked out an almost blue for the walls and a snow white for the trim. Her last stop was for overall cleaning supplies. Just as she was about to leave, she saw the Christmas decorations and, as a whim, she picked out a wreath for her new front door. She chose one that fell in line with the blue and silver of the town's decorations. It was fake but it had battery operated LED lights embedded in it. It had a small, metal Texas attached to it. She had escaped to Texas and this wreath would be a symbol of her new beginning. It was simple, but charming.

A shopping spree at Walmart rounded out her trip and then she was headed back to Twin Creeks. But first, the bright orange of the Whataburger sign beckoned her to the drive-through window in Glen Rose. She sure was proud of how productive she'd been today. She'd likely be home and unloaded by three. Her early start and run had been a perfect way to begin her new life. Sandy told herself this was a good habit and one she would try to keep up.

The café at six was Sandy's next appointment. She set an alarm on her phone so she wouldn't be late. She prided herself on being on time or early. After lugging the supplies to clean and paint up to her fourth floor, Sandy sat in the middle of her soon-to-be apartment and just dreamt for a minute about her new digs. As she surveyed her new bedroom and office, she realized that there wasn't much in the realm of actual remodeling to do in here. A deep cleaning and a fresh coat of paint was all it needed. This part of the hotel was hers alone to redo.

After a few much-needed swipes of the broom to get the cobwebs off the angled ceiling, Sandy was ready to put down a least one coat of paint and see whether she liked it. She was sure that these walls hadn't seen paint in forever. There were a few boxes that had been left here that needed to be taken downstairs on her next trip. Taping the windows and trim took the better part of an hour. Sandy rolled on the first coat of the barely blue paint. She knew that the trim would take time and would look better done in the morning with full light. Her phone chimed and with a quick check, she saw she had thirty minutes until she was to meet Fred, the handyman, at the café. Sandy cleaned the roller in the cute, old fashioned bathroom and headed down to the kitchen with two boxes and a suitcase in tow.

Since the cable guy would come tomorrow, she would use these boxes as her entertainment this evening. She had a good book as a backup if the boxes and suitcase were duds. Cleaned up and ready with a notepad in hand, Sandy started for the door. Time to meet Fred. As she cruised by the table, she knocked the bigger box labeled Pearl Beer Distillery to the floor and a pile of old photographs cascaded everywhere. These treasures were old, like turn-of-the-century old.

Sandy couldn't wait to look through them, but for now they made it back to the table and no farther. She'd be late if she stopped now to look at them. Out the door and beelining to the café like a woman on a mission. Well, she was on a mission. Sandy was hoping that Fred would work out. She was good at doing most of the work herself, but there was a lot to do to get this place up and running, and she would need the help.

The café was brimming with people tonight. Sandy learned that Monday was fried chicken night, clearly a crowd favorite. Although she was here to meet Fred and talk about her plans, and she bought plenty of food from Walmart, she felt like eating and the chicken smelled heavenly. Plus, it wouldn't hurt to begin to blend in with the locals. Martha pointed out Fred at a table by the corner window and Sandy headed over to introduce herself. As she approached, she had an uneasy feeling about him. He looked so Italian, like he could be related to Pete, just older like an uncle. All that worry stopped when he stood at her approach and opened his mouth. His west Texas draw was so thick, you would have thought he was straight out of a Louis L'Amour western novel. "Howdy, ma'am. I'm Fred Wilson. I understand you're the new owner of the hotel and may be in need of some help."

He motioned for Sandy to join him and did not sit until she was safely seated. "Yes, Martha recommended you to me. I've taken a few pictures of the rooms I want to work on first.

If all works out, I'll likely need you every day for a month or so. Are you familiar with the property?"

His face brightened with the mention of a month of work. "Well, little lady, as it so happens, I am available. Work is slow around here during the festival and the holidays, so I'm at your disposal. I've only been inside the hotel once and it was long ago."

Sandy smiled at his easy straightforwardness. Just another charm of this town, or is it the renowned Texas charm? "Here are pictures of what I want to start with. The lobby is a cleaning job and I'm sure I can find some help with that, but the front door and rear doors need new locks. I don't want to damage the antique doors for security sake, so I need your expertise on that. In the little library and reading room off the main foyer, the ladder that should roll doesn't, and all the tables need tending to. They're wobbly. The tables in the dining room are in the same shape. I'm going to shop for some chairs for those tables. I want them to be from the same period, but I know an exact match is impossible. Then, there's walls needing repainting, and the hardwood floors probably need sanding and refinishing."

Fred studied the pictures and looked up with a serious look that tells Sandy that he was excited to work on this project. "I love the thought of getting my hands on that lovely old building. Martha told me about the project and I did a little checking around. The electrical wiring in the building was updated not too long ago. An investor had that done, then disappeared. With that update, you will not need a larger fuse box so that is a big relief. Rewiring can be costly. The plumbing is ok, too. That last owner had it checked out, not to mention the inspections that were required when you purchased it. Mary at the bank has a folder about all the inspections done waiting for you at her desk."

Sandy tilted her head, questioning him and he answered as if he had read her mind. "Mary is my third cousin, once removed, if you're wondering and her sister is… well… my girlfriend. You reopening the hotel is big news in these parts. The old girl is a beautiful building and adds to the charm of our central city area. The tourists will really enjoy stepping back in time by staying at your place. I'm sure the paper will be around to write about it." When Fred mentions a news story, Sandy retreats to her safe place and sort of leans back in her chair. Sandy saw he noticed her uneasiness. Uncle Bob assured Sandy that this town was so far off the map, that the reopening of an old hotel would be in the papers but not make it back to the east coast. The mention of a news story did jingle her chain and make her want to hide. Sandy took a deep breath, straightened her posture, and smiled.

"There is so much to do and I'm not so sure I want reporters or photojournalists in our way, but we'll see. Have you eaten, because I am about to order the fried chicken special, how about you?"

With a wave of his hand, Martha was at the

table taking their order. While they waited for their meal, Fred and Sandy go from room to room and talk about her vision and color pallet. Not having her printer yet, it arrives in the morning, they have to share her tablet to look at the photos together. So, when the meal arrives their heads are together looking at her tablet. Martha, the owner of the cafe looks over Sandy's shoulder as she delivers her dinner. "I cannot wait to see what you two do to the place. I know that place has history and I can't wait for it to open." The second plate is delivered to Fred and the aroma is amazing. Fred didn't even answer her, he had a bite in his mouth before she finished her sentence. Instead of a verbal answer, he nodded and smiled. Sandy took a moment to thank her and ask for more napkins.

Dinner over and plans to meet in the morning, Sandy was more than satisfied to trek back across the courthouse lawn to her soon to be Grand McCormick Bed and Breakfast.

The moonlit evening enhances the hotel's, no B&B's, lovely old-world charm. The view is picture-perfect, kind of like an old Christmas card. If it snows, she would come back to this spot and capture the charm she saw now. This makes Sandy stop and do just that, take a photo for her future website. A trip to the library, or rather the LA, is another thing to put on Sandy's to-do list. She needs to put some time into research. The small amount of info she got from Uncle Bob was not enough for her. When cable is installed tomorrow, she could then connect to the internet to continue her research.

As she steps in and locks the beautiful antique front door behind her, Sandy remembered the boxes and suitcase in the kitchen. She retrieves them and takes them to her temporary bedroom to peruse through before she closes her eyes for the day. It's not long before she's knee-deep in old photos and souvenirs of a time at the turn of the century. The letters were addressed to EM. Was her name Emily, Eleanor, Elizabeth, Elaine? So many to choose from. Does the M stand for her last name? It was clear that the photos centered around a well-to-do, for that period, young woman probably in her late twenties. Although Sandy didn't look anything like this woman, she felt a kinship with her. In the suitcase were clothes of that time. All but one were conservative, lacey blouses and long skirts worn in the early years of the 1900s. One dress was so different. It looked like pictures Sandy had seen of the Roaring Twenties. It was black, with beads and fringe all over it. It was exactly what Sandy would envision a flapper wearing. Sandy had once dressed as a flapper for Halloween. Hers was a cheap imitation. This was the real deal. She loved these young Western women of the 1920s who wore short skirts, bobbed their hair, listened to jazz, and flaunted their disdain for what was then considered acceptable womanly behavior. Who was this woman? Was this her hotel or did she work here? Research would answer those questions, she hoped. All she knew so far was that, until ten years ago, this place was owned by a McCormick. Hmmm, M could be for McCormick.

THREE

SANDY HAD IDEAS FOR EACH room and quickly put her plans on paper. With rough sketches assembled, Fred and Sandy finalized what she wanted and where to start. The lobby seating area, dining room, library and reading room, plus the new locks for the exterior doors, were to be phase one for Fred. Sandy's phase one was the fourth floor.

Fred made a few calls and had a quote for her within thirty minutes, which turned out to be well within her budget. "Fred, let's get this party started." He was tickled pink and whipped out a simple contract and filled in a few blanks for numbers, descriptions and names.

Contract signed, Sandy and Fred got to work. In their negotiations, Fred had added his girlfriend into the mix to clean. He said she would start the next day and he was off to pick up supplies from Home Depot. Fred was pleasantly surprised when Sandy explained she had already opened a commercial account for building supplies there. That made things easy.

Fred ordered what he needed right away by

phone and learned he could pick the order up around noon, a little over an hour from now.

Before he headed out, Fred told Sandy, "I have a buddy who owns an auction and antique house just a few miles northwest of town just inside the next county line past Dinosaur Valley State Park. I talked to him last night after you left and he said you should stop by and look at what he has before his auction tomorrow. His name is George, so ask for him and he'll show you what just arrived from the Dickerson's estate. Ol' Mrs. Dickerson had a lovely home two counties over and I'm told it was loaded with the perfect furniture for this place. She lived in the old large mansion all her life and her family before her. I think it should be worth checking out."

Sandy had just been wondering where to shop for furniture. She wasn't an online kind of shopper, rather a hands-on kind of shopper.

"Wow, Fred! As soon as the movers get here and get unloaded, I will go by and check. By then I'll need a break. I have a spare key to the back door. Do you think you will be back before me?"

Fred looked over his shoulder from where he was measuring the front door. "Nah, if you're not back, I'll just head over to the café. You can pop in and holler at me."

Fred was in his truck and leaving just as the movers arrived. For the next two hours, Sandy directed the guys on where to put things. Her bedroom stuff went all the way to the fourth floor so it could be set up as soon as possible.

When the movers finally finished, she signed all the paperwork and they were gone. Now she could go out to the auction house and see if this place had a pot of gold, or rather furniture, for her.

Just as she passed Dinosaur Valley State Park, Sandy focused on watching for signs to Gilroy's Auction House. Sure enough, there it was set back off the road. It was a big barn with several other small buildings grouped next to each other across the driveway from a big white ranch house. The gate was open and she could see a big open sign on the barn.

Stepping inside Sandy was immediately overwhelmed by the number of interesting things in here. To one side, up against the wall, were bleachers that provided six levels of seating. Those looked like they were used for his auctions. The rest of this enormous place was filled with everything imaginable, antiques to newer items. Before she could take many more steps, a low voice from behind her asked, "hey there, what can we do for you?" Sandy turned to find an older man in his sixties standing about three feet behind her with coveralls, a beard and a potbelly. This had to be George. Sandy turned and started to speak but he beat her to it. "Well, I reckon you must be the new owner of the hotel in town. Fred did a good job of describing you. Glad you decided to stop in."

Sandy extended her hand to shake. "You have a treasure trove! Is everything for sale or are some things reserved for the auction? And when is your auction?"

"Smart girl, I do have some things reserved for the auction, but if you see something that's marked for the auction let me know and I'll see if there's a solution. I'm flexible on most."

With that, George gave Sandy a short tour of the main building, pointing out that the other two had more treasures to look at. Sandy and Uncle Bob had financially planned for this moment, not only for repairs but for décor, too. This was Sandy's favorite part. The hunt for the perfect piece of furniture. She strolled through the main building and found three dressers and six end tables in no time. She snapped a photo and used her post-it notes to mark them. These would be perfect in the rooms on the second floor. Hanging high on one wall were eight chairs that could be used in the dining room. But her favorite treasure was an ornate chandelier for the foyer. It was beautiful and a surprise find. There was a serviceable one already hanging in her lobby but this one was spectacular. Its numerous crystal pieces attracted every small sliver of light in this old barn and bounced it around the room. It would be stunning in her lobby, a real show-stopper. Maybe Sandy should have Fred bring the one in the lobby out here to the auction house. Maybe George would trade. Walking through was slow. Sandy would take a few steps and just look around. If she went too fast, she'd miss some of the hidden treasures. After making a list, marking with post-it notes all she wanted, and taking pictures of her 'for sure' and 'maybe' purchases, Sandy decided to move on to the other buildings. Her front porch needed some furniture and it had to be perfect. In the first barn, she found bed frames and lamps and light fixtures. She snapped tons of pictures but wasn't worried about availability because none were marked for the auction. Some of the fixtures she would have to talk to Fred about. Sandy wasn't sure how costly it would be to bring the light fixtures up to code.

In the second little barn, Sandy found the perfect piece for herself. It was a fainting sofa in purple. She was sure the upholstery was new but the sofa itself looked old. There was another small sofa and chair next to it that would look lovely in the foyer. In the excitement of her find, she spoke to the room, "Oh, I love these treasures! But no prices?" To her shock, an answer came from somewhere in the room. "Those are George's favorites, but he'd sell them."

Sandy whipped around to find absolutely no one there. Well, this was unnerving. Where did the voice come from? She heard a chuckle from above. Sandy slowly looked up to find a gangly girl perched on the beam above her. This girl was all legs and arms, and looked to be about thirteen. "Hi there, is George your dad?" The girl just stared. Sandy tried again, "my name is Sandy. What's yours?" Nothing…. "I sure could use an assistant who knows where all the good stuff is." Without a word, she dropped to the floor right in front of Sandy with such ease you knew she had done this a thousand times before.

"My name's Jane and George is my uncle. I do know where all the good stuff is. Are you the new hotel owner?"

Sandy rolled her eyes. "Does everyone know about me?"

"Yes ma'am, they sure do." Jane turned. "Come this way to the good stuff. It's back here."

With those words, she was off. Jane slid between two tall chifforobes and seemed to disappear. With a little work, Sandy squeezed through to the other side and behold there was a room full of amazing finds.

Jane stepped forward. "Don't you just love them? I bring the good stuff back here for me. Uncle George doesn't remember most of this stuff is here. I love old things and I love to decorate rooms. I think you would really like most of these treasures in your hotel."

Holy cow, this girl was right. This was the good stuff. What would George say about her hiding all of these lovely things here? Sandy was snapping photos, making notes, using her post-it notes. She turned and beamed at Jane, who had sat down on one of the lovely chairs.

Sandy had everything photographed that she was interested in and sat down next to Jane. "Does your mom know where you hang out? And will your Uncle George let me buy this stuff?"

A shy smile spread across Jane's face, "I don't have a mom, and George will let you buy it if I can come and help put it in the hotel. Uncle George and Aunt Sue adopted me after they found me at a car crash. I was eight months old, so I don't remember a thing."

Sandy could see the sadness in her face. "You are one lucky girl to be found and wanted. And they are lucky to get such a talented girl. Win… win."

Knowing her words would make this young girl happy, Sandy added, "You are always welcome to help, with or without the sale. You do know that the old hotel is going to be a bed and breakfast, so I have remolding to do first. Even if I bought the stuff today, I will have to wait to get it delivered when the place is closer to being ready. As far as helping at the B&B, don't you have school? And how would you get there?"

Jane jumped up and hugged Sandy as though her life depended on it. "Thank you! Yes, I heard that it was a B&B, but I don't know what that is. I can wrap these treasures up and get them ready to go when you need them delivered. I do go to school, but there's after school and weekends, and the Christmas holiday is right around the corner. I have a bike and with the festival, my aunt will go to town every day. Oh, thank you, thank you!"

Sandy liked this waif of a girl. "A B&B is different than a hotel because it's usually run by the owner, and a boutique hotel generally has a staff on duty 24/7. At a B&B, the owner usually lives on the property and serves at least breakfast to the guests. I'm living on the fourth floor, and floor one, two, and three will have guest rooms.

Does that make sense?" Jane nodded.

Just as Sandy was going to tell Jane she needed to talk to her uncle and get back to town to meet Fred, she heard her name. "Miss McAllister, you in here? Hellllooo?" Jane beats Sandy to the response. "Hey, Uncle George! We're way in the back. Be right out." Jane waved at Sandy to follow, so she does. Sandy could hear George muttering things like, 'what was she doing in there?' and 'nothing much back here, the good stuff was in the big barn' as we emerge behind him.

"Land sakes, you gonna scare a man to death! What have you two been up to?"

Again, before Sandy could answer, Jane announced, "Oh, I found her in here lost so I was helping her to find the way out when you called. She took some photos of some old junk back here she wants. God knows why. I told her since I knew where they were, I would wrap them up and get them ready for delivery. Oh, by the way, she needs us to hold onto them for a short time until the hotel, uh, B &B is ready."

All George said was, "Okay." Sandy guessed he was used to Jane's ways and didn't argue.

George and Sandy headed back to the big barn to make a list and nail down the cost of all these lovely treasures. Jane had copied the list and was off to begin putting it all in the same spot for packing and delivery. With goodbyes said, Sandy was on her way back to town to show Fred what she had found.

Sandy could see Fred's truck in front of the

hotel and he was sitting on the tailgate, waiting. She pulled up and popped out of her car. "Hi there! I hope you haven't been waiting long. There was so much to look at out at the auction house." With that, she sat down next to him on the tailgate to show him pictures of what she had purchased.

Fred was impressed with her treasures and thought it was funny that Jane showed Sandy her private stash. He was even more surprised that Jane let her buy it.

Sandy jumped down from the tailgate and headed for the front door. Fred followed, speaking to Sandy's back. "I want to unload supplies and get a few hours in, then my girl wants to come by and clean for a while. Is that okay with you?"

Sandy fought with the lock on the door. With further inspection, she realized it was different. From behind, "you'll be needing this new key since I already changed all the locks on the outside doors. I discovered that any child could get in here with the old locks in place."

Sandy took the key, smiled, and let them in. As she turned to wait on Fred, she sees that he was waving her back out to the porch. Sandy set her packages down and returned to the porch.

"Do you see the little black box attached to that light fixture? It is a security camera that is activated by a motion detector on your new doorbell. There are cameras on the back doors, too. I know you didn't ask for one, but with you up on the fourth floor, I figured you might really benefit from this high-tech gizmo."

This kind of thoughtfulness and insight was just what Sandy needed. "Fred, you are amazing and I can't tell you how pleased I am that you did this. Is there an app that I need to download?"

Fred smiled and put his hand out beckoning for Sandy to hand over her phone. "For now, I have the app on my phone, too, so I can see when a delivery arrives. I have one of these doorbell things on my home, so I can show you how it works."

This new addition to the front and back doors was surely what dad or Uncle Bob would have recommended if they were tech-savvy, but Sandy was so grateful Fred was up to date on this stuff. With the app loaded and a few instructions, Fred and Sandy practiced with it for a while.

Practice ended when Eleanor, Fred's girlfriend, arrival to clean and Sandy excused herself to work on the fourth floor and her soon to be sanctuary. She bounded up the stairs with a new sense of safety and control. With the bedroom things piled in the center of the floor and covered with a painter's cloth, Sandy put on a second coat of paint and then sat down to trim in the baseboards. Fred arrived with a ladder and began to work on the crown molding.

"I didn't expect to see crown molding up here," he said. "I kind of thought this might have been where the servants lived, so no need for fancy molding up here." Sandy stayed focused on her painting but added, "I wondered about that, too. I think the original owners lived up here at first. Maybe later, the staff lived here. Whatever the reason, it's beautiful."

Sandy had her favorite music playing in the background, so they both focused on the job at hand. A late night and early morning of intense painting and cleaning, then arranging the furniture so she could move up here for good had Sandy stretched out on the bed. Fred had checked on her several times after he finished the crown molding and she planned on joining him with the work on the first floor after lunch. Sandy collected everything from the downstairs bedroom and lugged it all up to her new space.

Lunch was all she could think about. A trip to the café was in order. It had been two days since she'd journeyed out. A good home-cooked meal was in order and the café had plenty of that. As she reached the lobby, Sandy peaked in the kitchen to see Frank and Eleanor enjoying a lunch at the kitchen table.

Standing there, Sandy realized this little workforce here in this room felt right. "Hi Eleanor, Fred. Your work looks good. I'm heading over to the café for lunch and will stop at the library on the way back, if you need me. I'm so glad the two of you took me up on the offer to stay here whenever you don't feel like making the thirty-minute drive to your house. It just feels right when you both are here. Do you need anything while I'm out?"

Eleanor answers first, "We're just fine. This ol' place is so charming and comfortable to work in, thank you for letting me be here." Fred turned his head and with a mouth full of sandwich struggles to say, "You mean 'this ol' place' is what makes you happy and not me? Dang, I guess I need to think about that."

This silliness earns him a cute smile and a kiss on the cheek, "While you think about that, mister, I have things to do." Eleanor grabbed Sandy's arm and they walked arm and arm to the lobby.

"I've cleaned and polished all the woodwork in the lobby. I was going to get on a ladder to tackle that light fixture up there, but Fred said the chandelier is being changed out. If that's the case, I'd like to clean the new one before it's installed." Sandy couldn't tell if Eleanor was just concerned or unhappy about the new chandelier. Just as Sandy opened her mouth to speak, the doorbell rang, then her phone, the phone in Eleanor's hand, and Fred's as he appeared in the doorway from the kitchen all sounded off with alerts.

"Yikes, we have a symphony of chimes with this doorbell gizmo!" Sandy exclaimed jokingly. Sandy opened the door to find Jane and George waiting to be let in, holding the skeleton of the chandelier and a box of crystals.

A little commotion later, the new antique chandelier was up, naked and waiting to be dressed with the crystal pieces Jane had carefully packed for the trip. Eleanor asked Jane if she could stay and help put them back on it after each one was washed and dried. Jane was beaming as the two disappeared into the kitchen.

Fred was still on the ladder checking the

connections and wanting the switch turned off and on when George turned to leave. "Thank you, George, for the chandelier delivery and allowing Jane to come here. We'll take good care of her. When does she need to be home?" Sandy loves the caring way and kindness of the people in this town.

George turns and chuckles, "she might outstay her welcome, so call if she does. Sue and I will be in town later for dinner at the café. We can get her then. She knows when to come over to the café. Have fun with my teenager." He was gone in a blink of an eye. Sandy stood by the switch as Fred came down from his perch on the ladder. "Go eat now while those two are busy. If you don't, one of them will rope you into something else."

With that advice, Sandy was out the door and on her way across the courthouse lawn to the café. Sandy stepped inside to the laughter of a group of young women who were sitting at the same table the magazine-ready men were that first night she was here. There were four women and they all looked about the same age as she was, mid to late twenties.

Vanessa hurried over to her as she sat in a booth by the door. "What can I get you? Our Wednesday special is meatloaf with mashed potatoes and corn. Can I start you with some sweet tea?"

"The special and a sweet tea sounds perfect. I'm famished." With Sandy's order in hand, Vanessa heads back to the kitchen to put it in and get Sandy some tea. Sandy watched her for a moment then was distracted as Jon the librarian stepped through the door and after pausing to take in the room, came straight to her table. Loudly he hollered, "Hey, Vanessa? Bring me the special and a tea, please." He looked down at Sandy, "Can I join you?" His smile was hypnotizing and completely unrefusable.

"Sure. I was going to stop by the library after lunch." Sandy glanced around and started to feel a little self-conscience with all the eyes locked on them. She still had not gotten used to everyone knowing everything.

Jon didn't miss a beat. "Lucky me, I get to see you twice. What are you having?" He noticed Sandy looking over his shoulder and his head whips around to the table of women. They were all still staring. "Rocky, get your reporter mind on your girl talk and off this table. We are like you and your friends, enjoying a meal together and getting ready to talk about research, nothing newsworthy... Yet." Jon wiggled his eyebrows up and down and all the girls at the table giggle, then conspicuously look away.

Rocky gave him a not so lady-like gesture and all the girls giggled again. Sandy was aware that any conversations she had with anyone could be considered newsworthy in this small town and that was okay, as long as it was just small-town gossip and not big city news.

Jon looked back and sighed, "that group was apparently thick as thieves in college and still is. Maybe they were all in a sorority together, or just roommates, I'm not sure. Rocky left for a while, I think to Chicago, but the rest are still here when she is here for the most part. They all have eyes on some of the prominent young men here in town, so be careful. Oh, and for the record, none are on me."

Sandy smiled an impish smile at him, "Okay, maybe after lunch you could introduce me to them... You know, get it over with. That way I can start to fit in. Who are they anyway?"

Jon's lips quirk up and to one side to reveal a devilish smile. "If you must know, Raquel Peake, aka Rocky, is a journalist, lately writing for some paper in Chicago, but currently home for the holidays, according to Owen. The one to her right is Lucy Loveless and she is a forensic accountant who, for a few years, was working in Houston but is visiting Rocky and using Rocky's parent's house as home-base. Not sure if she is here for good or what. To Lucy's right is Violet Starr and she works in the film industry, not as a performer but on the other side of the camera as an AD, an assistant director. Even though she has the right name for the acting side of the camera. To me, an AD really is just an over-titled and low-paid gopher. I think home base for her is Austin. but for now she is at Rocky's, too. The last one is Parker Jackson and she's a technical writer. I am not so technical, so I haven't needed to read anything she has written but she is always reading my books. That makes me happy. She's also at Rocky's parents big house just outside of town. All were in the same year in college, just different majors. All have decided I'm not their type and only eligible as good male friend material in order to get close to other male prospects in town. Sometimes I feel so used... So, I take every opportunity to tease them."

Sandy is stunned into silence. He's so candid. She did not expect so much information. Should this openness be thought of as creepy? "Uhhh, okay... On a different thread, what do you write, and do you have any of your books in the library? I would love to read them."

Jon nods. "Sure do and you sure can."

Their food arrives and the conversation stops for a few minutes. Both were happy to dig in and enjoy the meatloaf. It was a meatloaf roll of sorts. It looks like the meat was flattened and broccoli and rice were spread out on top then it was rolled up like you see jelly rolls made. It was delicious.

They both start to speak at the same time, then laugh. With a hand gesture, he encourages her on. "I found some pictures in the hotel of a young woman who was there about the time it opened. I would like to get some history on the place, just for me to know, but also about her if I can."

Jon's eyes light up with the news of the photos. "That is amazing. We do have some photos and info on the hotel and its owners along the way, but not much. I would love to see what you found. Are you going to frame the photos and put them in the hotel lobby? I think people will be surprised to hear how much history the old place has."

Sandy had planned on a visit to the library after lunch and now seemed like the perfect time to get his help. "I can go there now if you have a minute or two. I mean, I told Fred I was going to do some research there and be back by three. What do you think?"

Jon cuts his eyes to the table of girls and says softly, "If we leave together and walk to the library there will be talk. Are you okay with that?"

Sandy rolled her eyes. "Are we in sixth grade? I mean, I get that everyone knows everything about everyone here, and I'm trying to get used to that. Good thing I don't have a lot to hide." Sandy knows that was a big fat lie, but what could she say? She was hiding and she was trying to hide in plain sight. If that didn't work, then the offer for witness protection would have to be rethought. She gave herself a mental slap and waited for an answer. Jon is up and telling Vanessa to put this on his tab. Sandy said, "Oh, can I start a tab, too?"

Jon steps close to the counter. "She can start a tab tomorrow. Today, this is on me. Thanks, Vanessa."

Vanessa looked confused on what to do but Sandy nodded and all was well. Jon opened the door for Sandy and leaned close, "now the four at the table have more to talk about. I like that." Sandy was delighted with the devilishness and smiled back. "I would, if I were them. Let's make it good." Sandy smiled sweetly as she linked her arm through his and holds on to his elbow. He upped the ante and moves her arm behind him and puts his arm around her waist. They laughed as they walked hip to hip to the library. Sandy wished she could have turned and watched the reaction in the café, but having his arm wrapped around her set her girl parts on high alert. That was nice and truthfully all she could think about at the moment.

FOUR

AFTER REMOVING THE "CLOSED FOR Lunch" sign hanging on the front door of the library and unlocking the front door, Jon led Sandy to the archives room on the third floor. It had just dawned on her that the library was the only other building that had four floors like her hotel.

Sandy slid past a stack of boxes and over to a window that she thought might have a view of her hotel and Jon came to stand next to her. She was right, although the view was partially blocked by the fire escape attached to the library wall. She could see the back windows and the fire escape on her building. "I wonder if the fire escapes work…" she pondered out loud. "Hey look, there are two windows on my building that I didn't know existed. I'll have to look for them when I get back. Hmmm. One is on the third floor and one is on my floor, the fourth."

Jon answered, "well, I can tell you both fire escapes work because while the inspector was checking yours, he came over and wanted to see mine. After a good look, he said he hadn't seen this configuration in a long time. I wanted to know what he meant. So, he showed me. Wanna see?"

Sandy turned in surprise, "What do you mean?"

Jon headed for the stairs as he spoke, "I felt the same way, so I'll show you just like he did. Come on." Jon started up the narrow stairs to the fourth floor with Sandy trailing behind. As he climbed, he continued, "You see, when these were installed, they made them connect for safety in both buildings. This building was built a couple of years after the hotel and was a boarding house, not a fancy hotel. There were lots more people housed here than in your place. If there was a fire here, the likeliness of everyone making it down the one fire escape would have been slim. Here we are."

Jon was standing at a door that lead out to the fire escape. Sandy followed. As she stepped out onto the fire escape the whole thing groaned which made her pull back. Jon extended his hand. "No worries, I freaked out too, but he checked everything. It's safe." Sandy took his hand and stepped cautiously out and climbed the few steps to the roof.

Trying not to sound anxious, Sandy tried a joke, "Ok, what now? Do we jump to the other building for safety? Why in the hell would you climb up to escape a fire?"

Jon nodded. "That was my thought, too. Come stand by me. I'll show you why."

Sandy did and Jon unlatched a metal bar and

pushed. A long ladder-type thing began to swing out and stop just over the roof of her hotel. Then Jon lifted a rail on both sides of this ladder thing and pulled the bars up to reveal a handrail on both sides. This contraption spanned the alley four floors down. "Holy cow," was all Sandy could manage.

"Yeah, I know. It's so cool. The inspector said there's another one on your side for the same reason. It's just at the other end of this wall. You could go back and forth if needed." Jon was smiling like a man who had discovered a new ride at the amusement park, or a brand-new toy. As an afterthought, Jon added, "Oh, I'll have to go to your roof to swing it back."

Sandy couldn't think of a thing to say except, "Well, okay."

Back inside, Sandy stopped and looked around. There was something off in this room. It seemed too small for the roof she had just been on. "Jon, I think there is something wrong here. Is there another room up here? I mean, it feels too small based on the area of the roof." Jon turned in a circle and realized she was right. "I've never been up here, except with the inspector, but now that you mention it, I think you're on to something. That far wall should be farther away. Let's look."

A few minutes later and a lot of furniture and box moving, Jon and Sandy uncovered a locked door. Jon reached above the door jamb and retrieved a key that fit. Sandy was astonished and baffled. "Wait, I thought you said you didn't know that this existed?"

"Oh, the key... Sorry. When I got this job, all the doors were locked but had a key hiding just up above so I just assumed this would be no different. And here it is."

He turned the knob and they entered a large room that had three big windows that were boarded up. It was kind of dark in here with the windows blocked, so Jon searched for a light switch, found it, and switched it on, only to hear a bulb pop in the distance. Thank goodness, one bulb survived the ordeal. That still made this big place just dimly lit.

Jon took Sandy's hand and lead her in slowly. "Wow, what was this place?" were his first words.

Sandy was speechless. Before her looked like what she would call a loft apartment. No walls to define the space, just furniture to differentiate the kitchen from the living room and bedroom. The furniture in here had good bones, but every piece of linen or upholstery she could see were tattered and covered with layers of dust.

With that thought, Jon sneezed.

The only other door was small and on the same wall as what might be the bedroom. Sandy made her way carefully trying not to disturb too much dust so she could see where it led to. As she stepped through the door, she could see a stairwell about six feet in the front of her and what looked like a bathroom to her left.

The bathroom was surprisingly rather large but needed a serious remodel. There was an opening at the far wall that let you know it led to the big room on this floor. In today's designs, this would be called a Jack and Jill bathroom, which was basically a toilet and sink, then a door to the tub, then another door to a separate toilet and sink area. Sandy turned to Jon. "This is a nice sized bathroom and worth remodeling some time if you made it part of the apartment behind us. Let's find out where the stairs go." With that, Jon nodded and followed Sandy to the stairs.

The stairs were narrow and went straight down into the darkness at a steep angle. Jon was now standing behind her and a thought ran through her head. A person would not survive a fall from here, it looked like it went on forever without a way out. This thought made her sort of unstable and she wobbled. Jon grabbed her around the waist and pulled her to him. Oh God, she could have fallen. She turned in his arms but he continues to hold tight.

"Thank you, Jon. I almost fell." She said a little breathless. She looked up into those beautiful eyes and he smiled. "I wouldn't let that happen, but I certainly will let this." He leaned in and kissed Sandy. It wasn't an innocent kiss, but rather a lustful one. Sandy's mind ran the full spectrum of responses, but the one she went with the one her lady parts wanted the most. This man could kiss, and kiss him she did. As she deepened the kiss, he moaned and pulls her tighter.

Sandy had no idea how long this luscious kiss lasted, but she would remember it and revisit the pleasure running through her body later, in her dreams.

Jon turned them, moving Sandy from the edge of the dangerous stairs before releasing her. Still holding her by the waist, he kissed her on the forehead and said softly, "That was magnificent and we definitely need to do more of that, but for now I'll have to hope that you'll give me that opportunity later."

Sandy nodded and smiled. He was right, they would do this kissing adventure again, but later and not next to those stairs. Before she could answer, he had her hand and was starting down. It felt like the stairs were crossing the entire length of the building and down to the ground. When they got to the bottom, there was an unlocked door, but when Jon opened it there was a wall.

Jon spoke his confused thoughts out loud, "I think I know where we are, but there's no door on the other side." Sandy thought, how could that be? All these thoughts were running through her head as she was feeling the wall with her hands. "It looks like at some point it was plastered closed."

Jon was feeling all around, too, and finally stepped back, pulling her with him. He braced himself against the wall and kicked hard. You could hear things crash somewhere behind the wall. "Just as I thought, this is where the big bookcase in the lobby is, and it's not a permanent wall. Help me kick at it again."

Sandy was not willing to destroy old furniture. "What will it damage on the other side if it falls? We could go around and attack it from the other side."

In the shadowy light Jon tilted his head in thought, "nothing old or irreplaceable. Maybe a metal magazine rack." With that, they go at it... Two more times before it gives way. The noise of the bookcase falling was crazy loud. Just as Jon stepped through the rubble and turned to help Sandy through, Fred opened the front door of the library. "What the hell happened here? Are you two okay? Holy horse shit, there's a hole in the wall... No, wait... A doorway? Now, that's cool!"

Sandy stepped aside as Jon told Fred about the adventure of finding the apartment, the hidden door and the fire escape, only leaving out the lustful kiss. Sandy sat down because she knew this would take a minute. When all was hashed over, and Jon explained about the fire escape, they headed off to the roof here to investigate and learn more. Both men disappeared through the doorway and she could hear them climb the stairs.

Ten minutes later, both men returned to the first floor. Fred helped Jon set the bookcase upright and over to the side so the door would no longer be blocked. They all start to replace the books on the shelves, for now. Sandy was listening but was also thinking about the missing windows on her building. Well, they were really found windows, and she wanted Fred to see them, too. Sandy asked both men to go back to the window that faced her hotel. They followed, she pointed out the extra windows, and now all three were on to their next adventure. Find the windows.

Back in the lobby of the library, Sandy stopped at the rubble. "What about this mess?" Jon quickly wrote a note and posted it on the front door. "Closed due to renovations. Will reopen tomorrow at the usual time."

Sandy scratched her head, but followed. First stop for the boys was the roof of the hotel, but Sandy stopped at her place on the fourth floor and began to search for the extra window there. She opened the window closest to the corner of the library and leaned out. She could see it! She guessed that it was over near the closet, maybe in it. She opened the closet and had just stepped in when she heard the boys returning to help her solve the mysterious window issue. Sandy had not put her closet in order yet, so it was easy to see the slight difference in the far wall. How did she miss that when she was painting? Then it hits her. She did this part late at night.

Fred whipped out a hammer from his belt and swung it at the wall. His hammer easily sunk into the wall and a crash of glass was heard. "Oh shit, I should have taken that a little slower. Good news is, I can fix broken glass. I think." Both men put some muscle into this and had most of the temporary wall down that had covered the window in minutes. In front of them was a magnificent window seat. The cushion on the window seat was mush when they attempted to move it, and the boxes stacked on the seat itself were moved to the outer room.

Sandy just stood there in awe of this gorgeous

window seat. It was what every heroine had in turn of the century books. Sandy had always wanted one after she saw one in a movie. It was in an attic, high above the troubles of the world, just like this one. She couldn't wait to use it.

Jon stepped back and said, "Just like in the storybooks. Shame it's in a closet."

Fred, the ever-thinking handyman, said, "That's very fixable and with not too much work. This closet was an add-on because back in the day, permanent closets were not put in bedrooms. You used a chifforobe. You know like the one the kids cross through in The Lion, the Witch and the Wardrobe book?" A chifforobe is a southern term for a wardrobe. These two walls are not load-bearing walls and can be removed. We can build a nicer closest against that wall, or even a freestanding one where the closet is on one side and the headboard of the bed is on the other side. I have some pictures of one like that in my design book in the truck."

Sandy was thinking, 'this old-fashioned handyman has a design book' when Jon says it for her. "Well, la di da, you have a design book. Soon you'll be telling me you studied in Paris, and I don't mean Paris, Texas."

Fred sort of huffs, "House design and history are a hobby of mine. And no, I did not study in either Paris."

Sandy put her hands up to stop this craziness. "I want to see your ideas because that closet has to go… I want the window seat."

All three go back to the lobby with their news.

Eleanor and Jane were hanging what looks like the last of the crystals up on the chandelier. With a wave of her arm Eleanor announces, "Step back everyone, the light bulbs are in and all the crystals are in place. Jane, will you do the honors of flipping on the switch. Let's see what we've done."

Jane flipped the light switch, took it all in and clapped. Everyone quickly followed her lead. Sandy loved what she saw, but couldn't find her words. Fred broke the silence, "I'm so glad you had me install this here, and I hope you'll let me put the smaller ones at the top of the landing just up there." He points to a place just at the head of the stairs on the second floor.

Sandy just stood there as tears streamed down her cheeks. Jane's expression went from delight to concern. "Miss McAllister, I mean Sandy. I'm sorry, I should have realized you would want to be the first one to do that!"

Sandy looked surprised and turned to Jane. "No, that's not it at all. These are happy tears. This is just the first of many goals met and it's so exciting that it's happening. These tears are tears of joy. All of you are just amazing. Thank you, and yes Fred, put the other chandelier up there. It will be perfect there."

Some customs span the world, and hugs all around happen quite often in Texas, the friendly state. The completion of the chandelier was a great way to end the day. After everyone left, Sandy found herself in the kitchen fixing a simple dinner. She put it all on a tray to take up to her world on the fourth floor.

As she sat down at the table in her little place, she realized she had another surprise. The cable/internet guy must have come and gone because the flat-screen TV was on the wall and seemed to be hooked up. A large remote was laying on the table and, now that she thought about it, the small flat screen she'd bought from Walmart was hanging up in the kitchen, too. Sandy grabbed her laptop, checked the booklet left on the table for her password, and logged in. After an hour of chasing different stories about her hotel, she had copied and pasted all the important stuff into one document. The hotel was owned by the McCormick family from May of 1916 through 2007, when Maybelline McCormick passed away at 88 with no apparent heirs. The will said her estate should go to her sister-in-law's only child. She still hadn't found her girl in the picture, but her eyes were too tired and sleep was upon her. She would work on this again another day. Sandy closed up her laptop and snuggled into her cozy bedsheets and disappeared into her dream world.

FIVE

SANDY WOKE UP TO A bright, sunny day, but she knew outside had to be cold because the room itself was cooler than normal. Fred had taught her in these first few days to listen to the weather reports and understand that Texas weather changed with the flip of a coin, especially out here with no mountains to block the wind. Last night, the local news forecaster explained that this area would have a northerner blow in, changing the temperature quickly and leaving us with a crisp, clear sky. This could last for three or four days, according to the news, which had the town excited. This being the last weekend of the winter festival, Dueling Dinosaurs, people would come to enjoy the festival and this pleasant weather.

Next year, her B&B would be up and running, but until then she'd take her time to figure out how she could join in and be a part of this winter festival. Soon, Sandy would be welcoming a guest, Rocky's friend, to the room behind the kitchen. Rocky had no idea of how long or exactly when, just that her friend needed a comfortable place to stay.

Having her first real guest was a fun surprise. Even though Sandy was not charging regular rates, it was still income that truly made her feel this was happening.

Her guest, Madeleine Mitchell, should be here sometime between now and New Year's Eve, so getting up and dressed sooner each morning, rather than later, was going to be important. Sandy could hear Fred working somewhere in the building below. Eleanor had a booth at the festival, so she wouldn't arrive to check on him until much later. After touching the window with the palm of her hand to confirm just how cold it might be outside, Sandy figured this was a jeans, layered blouse and sweatshirt kind of day. Oh, and the new cowboy boots she had added to her wardrobe. She needed to break them in by wearing them every day, her instructions according Jon.

Sandy had taken to locking her apartment door after she found Jane sitting in the middle of her bed, rummaging through the box of old photos of the hotel. She liked Jane a lot, so rather than scold her, she just decided to lock up the room when she left it. Her explanation to Jane about that decision if questioned would be that there were too many workers in the hotel and her place was off-limits to any of them. That explanation should work, for now.

As Sandy arrived at the second-floor landing, she stopped for a moment to survey the progress of the place. Her lobby, which was large for this style of building, now sported a new wool rug in shades of blues and purples with a splash of red, so luxurious and welcoming.

The deep blue velvet brocaded fabric of the sofa and love seat together with the rich browns and oranges of the highly polished burl oak antique pieces made a beautiful picture of times gone by. The chandelier was sparkling and throwing bits of light across the room. This elegant sitting area and check-in desk gave a vibe of a peaceful place of yesteryears, with only the flat screen behind the check-in desk and the computer used to check guests in as evidence of the modern world outside the front door. The addition of the luxurious pull back drapes on each side of the door allows just enough light in without making it too bright inside on these west Texas cloudless days. It also adds much-needed privacy from any prying eyes on the porch. The porch, with its rockers and cushioned chairs, were a destination in itself and great for an afternoon respite from the sun and a lovely refuge in the evening from the prevailing west winds.

Sandy had enjoyed the wrap around porch for afternoon tea and late-night drinks with Jon. She had also added a trunk full of beautiful wool throws to be brought out to the porch for a chilly morning or evening rest.

Sitting in the lobby was Jane, curled up and reading. This intuitive young girl was just the person to get help from and show her the almost ready rooms.

"Hey, Jane! My plans today are to move the

newly acquired outdoor furniture to the second-floor balcony above the entrance to the hotel. You wanna help? Each of the two grand suites that face the front of the hotel on the second floor are almost ready to be put together, bedspreads and all."

Jane jumped up. "Yes, yes! I'm here reading, just waiting for you. Getting the porch… uh… balcony furniture out there now will be easier than bringing it through a crowded furnished room."

Sandy's original idea for these first two suites at the front of the second-floor had worked out well, with Fred's guidance. It was suite number three, the honeymoon suite on that same floor, that had changed big time.

Jane and Sandy carefully put the outdoor furniture into the small postage stamp of an elevator. "Jane, we are going to set up the two suites after we get this furniture out on the porch. Can you help with that, too?"

Before the elevator door was completely closed, Jane was already running up the stairs to see it open. "Yes…Yes…Yes… I am all in." Sandy on the other hand was just a little slower. "Hey, save your energy! We have a lot to do yet."

With one balcony of outdoor furniture in place, Jane turned to Sandy. "What do I do with these?"

"Oh, those cushions belong on the chairs on the balcony, but will stay inside in the trunk in each room unless the room is occupied."

Jane returned inside with the cushions. "There

are two different colors… What's up with that?"

"The blue ones belong in here, and the others in the other suite down the hall. Let's put this room together first, okay?" Sandy loved that Jane was interested in everything going in here, and even appreciated her numerous "why's," too.

Just then, Fred and Jon appeared in the doorway. "Need help?" comes out in sync and both men laugh. "Yes, if you two don't mind. Jane and I put the outdoor furniture on the porch, so now we need the beds and big pieces put in place so we can decorate. All the stuff is here, we just need extra muscle."

With a few instructions as to what goes where, all four work together as a well-trained team and in a little over an hour all the heavy stuff was in place with no scratches on the floor nor anything broken.

Jane was the first to break ranks, and insisting that everyone take a break. She grabbed a cushion from the pile and texted Eleanor. "Let's enjoy the view! Eleanor will be bringing drinks and a snack up to see what all the ruckus is about." With a cushion under her arm, Jane steps out on the balcony and picks out a chair, places the bluebonnet print cushion down and sits.

Sandy and the others follow her out. "This is a great idea! Let's take a minute to enjoy the view. It might be too cold out here, but we can try." Time was a wonderful commodity here in this small town and it was so different from the fast pace life in D.C. Sandy loved it.

Eleanor arrived with goodies, but refused to

stay on the balcony. "It is too cold out there! Can we stay in side?" Eleanor then shyly asks, "I noticed that the bed linens and drapes are different colors and Fred put nameplates on each door instead of numbers. Can you explain it to me? It seems confusing." Eleanor set the tray of cookies and drinks on the coffee table in front of the love seat and sat down to wait for an explanation.

"Yeah, I noticed that too. I thought hotels decorated each room the same." Jane added as she retreated inside with the others and then as an afterthought, "each room up here has a different color scheme and name... How come?"

Sandy held up her hands in a just wait gesture. "Well, in the spirit of a true B&B, each room is designed to have a personality. This suite is called the "Dickinson Suite" and is decorated in Bluebonnet blue, the state flower."

With the questioning tilt of their heads, Sandy continued hoping they would see the big picture. "The bed linens are a crisp, hotel white, with an extra quilt in a lovely shade of blue added at the foot of the bed on top of the white comforter. The walls are a very pale blue with crisp white crown molding. The artwork are historical photos of the room's namesake, Susana Dickinson. That framed painting is of the Dickinson home, just outside San Marcos on the San Marcus river and is to be above the headboard of the king-size bed in this room."

Sandy was so pleased that her audience was really listening. Jon had provided so much historical help. Jon smiled at her mentioning his help. "Jon's business contacts have helped me immensely with collecting historical stories and framing the artwork." Sandy's research had her take all that information and she had developed a nice brochure for the guests to read and take home as a memento of their visit, not only of the B&B but of the person whose room they stayed in. Each brochure would contain a short history and photo of the namesake.

Jane had moved to sit next to Eleanor on the love seat and she helped herself to more cookies. Sandy handed Eleanor her small tablet from the table. Jane scrolled through the brochure. Sandy told her little group, "I'm having them printed. This suite is two bedrooms and a small sitting area with a balcony over the front entrance of the hotel. Both bedroom areas are decorated the same and are meant to feel like you've stepped into Susana's home in San Marcos."

Sandy forges on because she thinks her audience was really listening and not just being polite. "Susana Dickinson, the namesake of this suite, was the wife of Captain Almaron Dickinson. She and her daughter were two of only a dozen or so survivors of the Battle of the Alamo. It's from Mrs. Dickinson that most of the first-hand historical accounts of the battle, from the Texans' viewpoint, originate. When Mexican general Santa Anna sent Susana to Gonzales with a letter of warning of what happened at the Alamo, instead of having the desired effect of intimidation, it became a rallying cry for the

Texas army. You know, 'remember the Alamo.' This army subsequently defeated the Mexicans at the battle of San Jacinto, even capturing Santa Anna himself. Susana was and still is a perfect example of Texan women, strong and proactive. There are several movies that Susana is portrayed in. Although she plays a minor role in them, for a woman of the time she is a good representation of the many strong women of her day."

Jane looked up. "That is so cool! I didn't know about her and I was born in Texas and have studied Texas history a lot. I think when I need to write a report for school, I'm going to choose her."

Sandy quirks her lips up in a smile. "Well, you might really like the namesake of the second suite better."

"Okay, shoot… Let's hear it… I sure like the first woman."

Sandy took a sip of her ice tea and pressed on. "The second suite, also in the front of the hotel, is just as lovely. It is dedicated to Angelina Eberly. Though not a native Texan, Angelina Eberly was a courageous woman and an important figure in Texas history. In December of 1842, Angelina made her mark on history when she fired a cannon into the General Land Office building in Austin, alerting the city of a theft taking place."

Janes eyes widen, "You mean, like a real canon?"

"Yep. The theft in question was being committed by none other than Texas governor Sam Houston himself, who was quietly planning to remove the Texas archival documents from Austin to Houston in an attempt to move the capital of Texas to Houston."

Jane gasped and Eleanor spoke for the first time, "Did she kill anyone? That sounds dangerous."

Sandy loved the drama and the Texas loyalty that this story evoked in her listeners. Jon already knew this story because he helped with the research.

"Angelina's efforts, which are now known as the Archive War, earned her the moniker "The Savior of Austin," and a statue depicting the famous cannon blast now sits in downtown Austin on Congress Avenue, between 6th and 7th Streets. Above the headboard in the first main bedroom of the two-bedroom suite will be a photo of the statue of Angelina Eberly in Austin. That room is mostly in shades of reds and pinks. Mrs. Eberly owned and ran the Eberly Inn where Sam Houston resided instead of the Presidential home afforded to him. Eberly Inn was at the time the nicest and most stylish place to stay in the village of Austin. Austin was a village back then, not the big city it is today. Sam Houston, being aware and concerned about appearances and fashion and political allies, wanted to be seen in the best places. Eberly Inn was that place. Her small rose garden just outside the carriage entrance to the Inn is the inspiration for the color influence for her namesake suite.

Jane slapped her thigh just like some ol' cowhand. "Another wild Texan woman. I'm so glad to know I'm not the only wild one around."

Everyone laughed at that declaration and Jane just rolled her eyes.

Jane nodded at Sandy to go on, "I know there's more to the story, Sandy."

"Well, yes just the description of the decor. The comforter is a beautiful impressionist print of red and pink roses. The walls are a barely pink color and dark wood crown molding like the furniture and floor stain with a striking rose red rug protruding out from under the beds. The print of the drapes and upholstery of the two chairs in the sitting area are also rose inspired prints. The antique furniture in this room is from your collection in the barn at the auction house, so Jane I guess you kind of inspired this room, too. The dark walnut in this room had to have traveled from far away to make it to Texas. Walnut like this, well, it's not native to this area. Angelina knew all about fashion for her time. There is a portrait of Angelina in the second bedroom of this suite, above the bed. I prepared a brochure on Angelina Eberly for the guests of that room, too."

Jane was so into listening that she waved her hands frantically. "What about the honeymoon suite? What are you calling it?"

Sandy knew that one still needed work, but the design and decór were already planned. It would just take time. With Jane's insistence she started again, "The first two suites took just removing some walls, painting and resurfacing the floors. The third suite, the honeymoon suite, or Happy Trails suite, has the most work to be done. Not only is a third bathroom to be installed at one end of the suite, but the window on the west side of the building needs to be completely redone."

The small sections of the big window in that room have been replaced at many different times and many years apart, and the formerly clear glass is now permanently many shades of yellow. The view from that window is such a stunning view and features a bird's eye view of the sunset, so the window's replacement is essential.

Fred stood and scrunched his eyebrows together, like he was thinking on a tough math problem. "You mean like Happy Trails, the song that actors Dale Evans and Roy Rogers made famous?"

"Actually, yes!" Sandy changed screens and a picture of Dale Evans popped up. Eleanor's surprised voice said it all. "Well, I'll be. I didn't know Dale was a Texan!"

"Yep! Dale Evans, was born in 1912 in Uvalde, Texas. She had a pretty chaotic life early on and she spent a lot of time living with her uncle, a general practice physician in Osceola, Arkansas. She was a real scrapper from all accounts." Sandy scrolls down in her research and points at the screen.

"Look at this. She eloped and married Thomas Fox when she was 14. They had a son when she was 15. A year later, her husband up and abandons them. So, she heads to Memphis, Tennessee, a single parent, can you imagine? She was pursuing her dream for a career in music. She got a job singing and playing piano for a couple of local radio stations. She finally divorced in 1929, and took the name Dale Evans to promote her singing career. I guess she was done with carrying around that baggage and wanted a fresh start."

Fred leaned in, "she sure is one interesting lady. I love watching the reruns of their TV show. So how and when did she find Roy Rogers?"

"Well now, that was fate. Republic Studios cast her as a singing cowgirl next to Roy Rogers and his co-star. The rest, as they say, was history."

Sandy loved this kind of stuff and, by Fred's interest, so did he. "Look here, Sandy. It says Dale married Roy on New Year's Eve in '47 at the Flying L Ranch in Oklahoma. That's where they had filmed Home in Oklahoma earlier on! Whewee, this marriage was his third and her fourth marriage, but it worked! They worked together on and off the screen from '46 until Rogers died in '98. They both had children from their previous marriages, and had one child together who died of complications from Down syndrome real early on. It says Dale's life inspired her to write a bestseller. And here it says a group in Oklahoma renamed after her because of her influence on early childhood mental illnesses and awareness."

Sandy smiled, in her heart and outwardly, at the memory of Dale's most famous song that she wrote, Happy Trails. "Here's that show you loved... 'They both starred in the highly successful television series, The Roy Rogers Show, from '51-'57, in which they continued their cowboy and cowgirl roles. In addition to her successful TV shows, she is known for more than 30 films and some 200 songs. She was inducted into the Texas Trail of Fame in 1997. She ranked No. 34 on CMT's 40 Greatest Women in Country Music in 2002."

Jane pointed at a quote enlarged on a page all by itself, "Is that from Dale?

"Yep! I am going to print it big, frame it and put it on the wall in the room. It seems fitting. 'Cowgirl is an attitude really. A pioneer spirit, a special American brand of courage. The cowgirl faces life head-on, lives by her own lights, and makes no excuses. Cowgirls take stands; they speak up. They defend things they hold dear.' I just love it!"

Fred looked around at all of us, "alright, this chatter isn't getting our work done. Even if it's pretty interesting. Let's get to it."

Sandy and the others got up and headed out to complete their jobs in different places in the building. Eleanor headed back to the kitchen; she had already planned to cook tonight's dinner for everyone. Fred went to check on the new bathroom being installed on this floor, and Jon said his goodbyes, heading back to the library for a while. As Jon started down the stairs, Sandy could here Eleanor tell Jon, "Supper is at seven, see you then."

Jane and Sandy went to finish, or at least put a dent into finishing, the Eberly Suite. They finished just in time to hear Eleanor ring her bell by the kitchen door. Sandy had almost removed it once because of where it hung. If she walked too close, she hit her head, but she decided its historical charm outweighed her head's safety.

With dinner over and the kitchen cleaned, everyone headed home. Sandy locked the doors and made her way to the fourth floor. Tonight, Sandy had made up just in time to see the last remnants of the sunset. It was a small blaze of orange on the horizon. It just made her stop in her tracks. After a moment of taking in the color of the sky, and the sweet silence of a small town getting ready for bed, her mind wandered to her past. This small town is just what she needed to get away and write. Maybe she would finally stop feeling like she was a part of the crime books she had lived in for the past five years, and more like a real person moving forward.

Maybe here, in her new sanctuary, she could force her demons to escape into the pages of her journal or maybe even a true-crime book. Maybe she could write about it and let it leave her and be captured on paper, like the shrink that her Dad insisted she visit suggested.

"Would it be dangerous to do that?" she wondered. "If I change all the names and write it like a novel, would a scary, suspenseful crime story in the first person allow the demons out and locked on paper?" She could start with a list of the crap that she witnessed or heard and see where it goes. A list might be all she needs to rid herself of the demons that haunt her dreams. Hmmm, a journal or a novel? As she headed to her bed, Sandy had the smallest hint of solace with her plan to write… and that was something.

Before her mind surrendered to sleep, she had a moment of warm memories of being in Pete's arms and then, just like a light switch flipping on, she relived the violent side of him. That scary moment returned when she inadvertently watched him brutally punching a woman in the gut. She had no idea why he did it, but that really didn't matter. It was awful. If he had seen her watching, would she have been next? Her heart wished one thing, but really, she knew in her soul that he would flip his bad side on her one day, too… Maybe not right then, but sometime.

Sandy's eyes popped open and she forced herself to come back to the present. She was not there with him. She gasped, she needed air. Sandy got up and splashed some water on her face, hoping she could try to sleep again. But first, she would try to make that memory leave her, through ink and paper. Something had to help. It took fifteen minutes to put it to paper, and two minutes to drift to peaceful sleep. Her last thoughts before sleep took her was, "this writing might work. I could put it on paper, make it stay there and not muddy up my peaceful retreat here in Texas." It needed to be out of her head, for good.

SIX

THE DUELING DINOSAURS FESTIVAL WAS something Sandy would have expected in Maine or Montana, or even Wisconsin, but not Twin Creeks, Texas. It started the day after turkey day and includes two fun weekends filled with your typical festival booths, parties, and events. The show stopper was the ice sculpture contest, and it was the most unexpected part. Texas weather does not always cooperate with cold weather so they had a contingency plan for a frozen tent just like the ice exhibit at Moody Gardens in Galveston. This year, Sandy was a spectator and participant, but next year she would have the B&B up and running, and hopefully full of guests.

As the days slide by and the festival comes to a close, it seems to have been a success. Eleanor operated a booth, and Jane's favorite part of the festival was the ice sculptures. It turned out to be Sandy's favorite, too.

Sandy's daily writing in list form seemed to help with the scary dreams. The writing had captured them on paper. She wanted them locked away for good. The front porch started as a great place to sit and write, but the last few days had progressively turned too cold for any porch sitting. Christmas was almost upon us. Most times, Sandy was either sitting in the kitchen if Jon was about, or snuggled in her window seat watching the world and writing.

It was too dangerous to visit Dad for Christmas, and too dangerous for him to be here. Thanks to the budding friendship and relationship with Jon, she wouldn't be alone. She was seeing him every day and had enjoyed many steamy kissing sessions. He seemed to be busier lately with the library, or was it his writing? Sandy knew that they had not spoken of exclusivity to each other, but for her it was already that way. Sandy had already in her head and heart moved to the next step in this relationship. She was keeping her decision to herself, even though Eleanor was trying to quiz her about him daily. She knew that if the right moment arrived for real intimacy she would fall right into his arms, no questions asked.

Today, Sandy needed to take photos of Fred's work. When the Grand McCormick B&B was completed, Sandy planned on sending her photo journal to a travel magazine. She has freelanced for them before and was sure that this article on the refurbished old hotel would suit their publishing mission statement. Not to mention, with her reputation for good, solid work, this article would satisfy their standards, too. Sandy would publish this under a new pseudonym for safety, even though she doubted that Pete and company peruse travel magazines. To stay safe, she would not use her real name.

There was a light snow falling and a cold, persistent wind blowing from the west. Sandy bundled up, cowboy boots and all, for the short walk to the library next door. She was returning Jon's book to him. Thank goodness these murder stories were not based on his real life, because this one was sort of scary for the detective. Unlike her writings, that were sadly all too true. Sandy had not let Jon read any of her writings, even though he was under the impression she was trying her hand at a fictional crime story. He wanted to read it but that made her nervous. Not because of the story, that was scary enough, but she was not sure what kind of storyteller she was when it was not about interior design and remodeling. Sandy had never thought of herself as shy but maybe about this, she was.

The story was a problem because, if he read it, he would sort of know her secret and she hadn't decided if she should open that door with Jon. In time, if things went well, she would come clean. But for now, she didn't want to scare this book-writing librarian away. Her world was all too real.

Jon was nothing like Pete. Pete's family was from Italy, specifically Sicily, and he had that alluring, sexy Mediterranean look. Jon had more of a rugged, Scottish look with a stockier build. Strong, big work muscles v.s. long, lean swimming muscles, both lovely. Sandy missed the sweet moments with Pete, but the cruel side of him really ended that fantasy of being with him forever. Pete thought differently, he had an intense possessive way which, at one time, Sandy had mistaken for love. His threats of violence were why she was here, not to mention her soon-to-happen court testimonial against him and his family. Dad and Uncle Bob, with the help of Bob's son Jamie, had arranged for Sandy's security since the group of criminals that Pete was a part of were notorious for destroying anything in its way, including her, since she was in the way.

Sandy was ready to hike over to Jon and return his book when her phone rang with an unknown number. She hesitated and decided to let it go to voicemail and listened in. The voice on the other end started, "Kayleigh? It's Jaime." Warning bells go off in Sandy's head. Jaime was using her real first name. He knows not to. "Kayleigh, are you there? There was a problem and dad asked me to bring the rest of the stuff you left here with him to you. It's a storage problem. He's not here right now and I need your address so I can get on the road. Call me back, or better yet just text me the address and I will put it in the GPS and start your way."

The phone goes dead and she hangs up. She's glad she let it go to voicemail. She turned the phone off and went straight to the computer and emailed her dad as per his instructions. Just an emoji of a frightened face. She logs out and turns off the computer, and even unplugs it. The burner phone she had just in case was in the vault in the storage room behind the front desk. She got it out, turned it on, and then stuffed it into her coat pocket. She sat down in the lobby to think. Dad would call this phone as soon as he could with any news. Crap, what was the next thing he said to do? This had spooked her big time. Oh yeah, find people to be with. Leave wherever you are and stay away until she heard from him. Okay, get to Jon.

Sandy had her coat on and got out the door, making sure to lock it up even though she knew Fred was still here working. Even though it was snowing outside, she practically ran to the library. Opening the library door, Sandy came in with a gust of wind and her personal snowstorm. Not just the one outside, but the one in her head. Be calm. "Hey there, Jon. It sure is windy out there." Sandy stomps her feet on the mat to shake off the snow and slush. "I'm going up to our little alcove on the second floor. I need a little quiet time. You, however are a nice distraction. So, come up when you can." Jon steps up close, helping with her scarf and using it to pull her into a lovely, warm kiss.

"Mmmm, you taste like a breath of fresh air. I want more." Sandy wanted more, too. She wanted to fall into his arms and just cry. She wanted to tell him everything. Could she? She could see him notice her shivering. "Sandy, you're shivering. There's a crocheted throw behind the counter, take it with you and wrap up till you get warm. I'll be up soon to check on you."

Sandy felt so scared but she needs to calm down first and think. No rushing into more trouble without a plan. Sandy smiled, leaned back a little and looks him over, then kisses him again. There was a clearing of a throat and both turned to see ol' Mrs. McDoogle wolfishly smiling at them. "Don't mind me, I'll just start putting books back on shelves. Mildred will be here soon. She's running a little late."

Mildred May and Mary Ann McDoogle were sweet ladies, roughly seventyish, who volunteered from ten until two, three days a week. Both worked here in their youth, had families, and now came to escape their retired husbands. If asked, they would tell you just that. With pleasantries exchanged, Sandy headed up to the second floor. As she climbs the stairs, Sandy struggled with what to share and not to share with Jon. Her friendship, no relationship, was wonderful and she wanted it to last. She needed to be honest, but there was only so much a normal man could accept. Her life had some really bad bumps in it, dangerous ones at that. And after that call, they may have found her.

This area on the second floor was open to the first floor and could have been a common room when this was a boarding house years ago. Sandy's favorite area was a secluded table in the far back corner. You could hear what was going on at the entrance but you had to listen and concentrate. Her hideaway had squeaky floorboards to warn her if someone approached, even though she couldn't see them through the shelves of research books and maps that surrounded her. Sandy's stomach was doing flip flops from the stress of the call.

Not too long after she was settled, when she was still trying to pour the scary phone call and yet another tarnished memory of Pete and his crimes into her journal, when Jon joined her. Her relief at his presence was tangible. They worked comfortably for a few minutes, then Sandy wanted another book to refer to which was up a floor. Jon offered to fetch it, but she needed to stretch her legs, try to think and keep her mind busy while she waited for the all-clear call. She unconsciously patted her pocket where the burner phone was located. There was a restroom on that floor, too. She needed to splash some water on her face. Maybe a trip in there would help.

Sandy sat in the stall and found herself submerged in her anxious, fearful thoughts. She was holding the burner phone, willing it to ring, but it didn't. It took her longer than she thought, to compose herself, because when she returned, she saw Jon holding her journal looking deep in thought.

"What are you doing?" She was close when she spoke and this made him jump and stammer to his feet. "I'm sorry, I just couldn't resist. It's good. I was so into it, I didn't even hear you approach, squeaky floorboards and all. I'm sorry I invaded your privacy. I was just so curious. Forgive me?" He reached for her, pulls her into his arms. Her anger recedes from wanting to hit him, down to mild irritation.

"I'm not sure I was ready for you to see that. I'm not an experienced writer in this genre. But I guess the cat's out of the bag. Since you've read it, I might be ready to hear your critique but be gentle." The kiss that follows was all the reassurance Sandy needed. So, as he sat and began to talk, she relaxed a little to listen.

"I've only read four or five of these scenes, and I wonder why you have them separated into a list rather than just telling us the story with you in it. Adding transitions from one to the other, and a written timeline incorporated in it, is all that's missing. It's a powerful story."

Sandy blinks. He means this. He was treating her as an equal, one writer to another. "Uhh, I thought I'd put the scenes, as you call them, down first and then weave them together."

Jon scratches his head. "That can work for research and the gathering of your thoughts, but I think it's time to use your tablet to begin the job of threading it into order. With a tablet, you can switch things around if need be for the sake of making the story flow better. Have you described the characters in your novel... like a list of who's who in the book? Is this true? I mean, it feels real."

Crap... Sandy likes this man, and even trusts him, but does she truly want to level with him? She didn't want to endanger him. As Sandy sat there thinking, she could see he was, too. Both lost in their own world. Just as she started to put him off, he speaks. "I think this is true and you're hiding. I'm not afraid to know. I investigate crimes for a living, you know for my books. With Dylan and the Stone brothers, there are so many stories I hear. I'm very careful. So, don't worry about me. I like you and hope this, whatever our relationship is, continues and gets stronger and better. Ok, save me from rambling on or before I put my small-town foot in my big mouth, cause I like us."

A huge grin, no full smile spread across Sandy's face. She could feel her tenseness recede. Slowly, she took his hands in hers and said, "I like us, too. If I tell you all, you would be in danger. I don't want that."

Jon sat up straighter. "So it is true. I just knew it. It rings true. You may see me as tame writer/librarian, but I can be a ferocious warrior and will be if this evil arrives here. I need to know who and what this warrior is protecting you from. I'll need to know the good guys from the bad guys."

Sandy couldn't help but giggle but then got serious. "Okay, but not here. Too many 'not so good at hearing' little ol' ladies about." She looked over his shoulder to a small shadow behind the second row of books. With an understanding look, Jon leans over and kisses Sandy, not a sweet peck but a lustful one. Then without turning, "Mildred or Mary Ann, whoever is eavesdropping, I hope you got enough gossip and sex lessons for one day."

A book hits the floor. "Well I never… Just shelving books here, when your story… Well, it sounded better than any book I'm shelving. You two have at it, but you might need a room from the flush on her face." Mildred walks briskly, for a plump seventy-ish woman, to the stairs and heads back to the first floor.

Jon stood and spoke quietly, "I was going to take you to lunch at the café, but I think fixing you lunch at my place sounds better, and more private."

Sandy looked up as she was collecting her supplies. "It's a long drive back to Glen Rose to your place. My place is closer and I'm sure we can find somewhere to be alone."

Jon laughed. "Right... between Eleanor and Jane, not to mention Fred, who by the way thinks of you like a daughter. He thinks you need protection from a big bad wolf named Jon. You really think we could be alone?"

Sandy shrugged. "Well, it was a thought." Jon stood very still for a moment, then nodded like he was talking to himself. "Grab your stuff, I have a surprise. Come with me."

Sandy was more than willing to follow but she couldn't resist the temptation to tease him a bit. "You mean I should follow the big bad wolf?"

He turned and grabbed her. "Yes, you should, so the big bad wolf can put a flush on your pretty little face again. Come on." He kissed her again and took her tablet bag and headed to the stairs. Sandy happily followed; she loved his surprises. She patted her pocket again in hope that it would ring. He was a nice diversion while she waited for her dad to call.

When he didn't stop on the third floor, she thought maybe he'd found more historical goodies about this town in the storage area on the fourth floor. Last time she was here, they found the abandoned apartment. She is surprised to see that he had been up here, cleaning and rearranging. Somehow, he'd found a desk and more bookshelves and had made himself an office.

"Wow, Jon this looks lovely. This is a long way to come just to work in your new office, but it is private."

He was standing with his back to the door of the abandoned apartment, overseeing his new office. "I found all this furniture up here shoved into corners, even these oriental rugs. Aren't they beautiful? This is part of my surprise and you're welcome to use it any time. You can even cross by way of the fire escape if you want. But maybe not on a day like today. With these high winds, it could be too dangerous."

Sandy looked toward the fire escape window/door, but couldn't think of a reason to do anything like that, so she just turned back, smiled and nodded. Jon had moved and opened the door behind him and she could see into the old abandoned apartment. It looked very different from when she was last here. It was bright inside, not from lights but filled with outdoor light. Jon beckoned her in and to her utter surprise, it was clean and Jon had moved in. This space was beautiful and not anything like the apartment he had in Glen Rose.

This apartment appeared, by its sophisticated look, to belong to a man of refined taste, not a college dorm room. Sandy loved what she could see. Jon was waiting patiently for her to say something. Sandy couldn't see very far in, but what she could see was simply beautiful. She could see a sleek kitchen that was once just a sink and a couple of cabinets. Now it was this modern, cutting-edge kitchen with all the appliances any chef would want. The windows were clean and the boards that had covered the windows were gone, revealing amazing views of the town and Texas countryside. Standing just inside the door was a free-standing wall that had a slim table and wall decorations that looked like dust covers of books. A closer inspection reveals that they are book covers of his books, no… wait, they say JR Wellman not Jonathan Wells. Jon points to something around the corner of the wall and Sandy followed as he disappeared.

Sandy rounds the corner to find a big picture window. "Jon, this is stunning and that window is the same view that I have from my window seat and the honeymoon suite. You've done exactly what I want for the honeymoon suite, putting the bed facing the window. When? How? This is a delightful surprise. I didn't think you had this in you."

Jon was sitting on the edge of a king size bed that faces the window waiting. He pats his hand for her to sit next to him. "My apartment in Glen Rose wasn't mine, just rented, and I knew it was ugly but after I saw what you were doing here I realized and was motivated to get on with my life and put down roots. Twin Creeks is where I want those roots to be. So, I went to the courthouse struck a deal with the county to buy this building and lease it back to the library for substantially less than the upkeep they spend. I asked Fred for advice and hired some of his friends to work on this apartment first. I intend on redoing each floor slowly. So, you like it?"

"All I can say is WOW. This has to have cost a fortune, not to mention the purchase of the building. But Wow."

Jon leaned in and kissed Sandy on the cheek. "You inspired me to grow up and use the money I've been saving from my book sales on this… My dream. Eleven successful novels and a television deal in the works had my savings account looking good. I don't have any family so I figured it's high time I work on something permanent for me rather than wander all the time."

Sandy was stunned, and realized that this man had many layers. So far, she liked what she saw. "I'm totally surprised, impressed and excited for you. I didn't realize you had so many books out. Is JR Wellman your pen name? The book you gave me to read had Jon Wells as the author. I'm confused."

A sneaky smile spread across his face. "You see, I wasn't sure how I felt about sharing my inner world… just like you, being ready for you to be in my world scared me. The book you had was the first book I wrote and then I went with a pen name. I was startled by your world when I was reading your journal. It made me realize that you and I are at a crossroads. We either trust each other with the real us or not. When you trusted me, I wanted you to see that I trust you. So here we are."

Sandy couldn't believe this beautiful man was opening his heart to her. She needed this and him. Jon's words were just what she wanted to hear. The scary call from the fake Jaime had her head swimming, not to mention that her dad still had not called back. Jon continued on, speaking softly to her. "I want and need you. I'm not sure if we're forever, but this… I mean 'us' is so good that I'm beginning to think so." Sandy's mind was running a mile a minute. She needs to let him know what's going on. How should she do this? How much can this author/librarian handle? His crazy moments were in his books, not real and lurking behind the next door like hers.

"Sandy, you're far away." Jon kissed her. "All I want to know is that you are interested in me enough to see where this leads us… permanent would be a fairytale for me, but for now I'm happy to escape to your world and be with you. Your knight, milady, needs to know what villains are about so he can protect her." Jon moved closer towards her and uses his strong muscles to place her firmly farther up on the bed. When he joined her, Sandy happily threw all of her focus and energy into a naughty kiss that morphed into the decadent, slow removal of clothes.

Sandy now knew she had to tell him. He was offering her shelter, a place to go for a mental rest. She would no longer need to do this alone. But her crazy world would have to wait a little longer. She gets him first.

For the next hour, give or take, there was no talk of villains or criminals, just hot, passionate sex. They lie there enjoying the comfortable, intimate silence after, when Jon's phone began to ring. Jon answered and Sandy is close enough to hear.

"Mr. Wells? Mildred here. There's a Mr. Smith, suspicious name, here at the desk. He says he's your publisher. Can you come down here? Oh, and Fred is here looking for Sandy. Can you put her on the phone?"

Jon replies, "Yes, I'll be right there. Give me five minutes." Then he hands the phone to Sandy as he starts to dress.

"Sandy? Where are you? I need to pay these guys and I have a few questions about the Happy Trails room." Sandy put the phone on speaker and starts dressing, too.

"Fred, you'll find the money in the vault, marked with today's date. I'll see you at dinner and we can go over the plans then. Okay?"

He responds with a drawled out ,"Great," and ends the call.

Jon starts for the door that leads straight to the first floor just past the bathroom, but Sandy stopped him. He thought it was for a kiss, but she sits him down in one of the kitchen chairs and pulls one up close. "Do you have a publisher named Mr. Smith?"

"Yes... Why?"

"Good... I mean, are you sure it's the right Mr. Smith?"

Jon was no dummy and Sandy's questions have a no-nonsense undertone... They make him anxious. "No more questions. I want answers. Spill, what is going on? You have been on edge since you got here. I thought it was because I read your journal, but there's something else."

Jon picked up his phone and sends Mildred a text, "Take a pic of Smith and send it to me."A happy emoji followed by a pic.

"Okay, it's my Mr. Smith so spill. I need to know." Jon texts Mildred, "tell Smith I'll be down in a few. Keep him busy." A happy face emoji comes back.

Five minutes later, Sandy had told him about the call and her fears and the email to dad and the burner phone and the fact that dad hadn't called back with the all-clear signal.

Without a word, Jon goes to the door of the apartment and puts the deadbolt in place and checks all the window locks, then returns to Sandy. She had started to follow him to the door but he signaled her to stay. Jon pulls her into an embrace and tops it with a sweet kiss.

"I'll be right back. You stay right here. This should take ten minutes, tops."

SEVEN

TEN MINUTES LATER ON THE nose, Jon was back and locked the door to the stairs behind him. Sandy, not knowing for sure it was him when she heard heavy footsteps, had taken cover behind the sofa. When he calls her name, she stands up and watches as he removes his weapon and lays it on the table. She didn't even know he carried.

"Please don't sneak up on me." Sandy sits down as tears start to flow. Jon scoops her up and carries her back to bed. He heads to the kitchen and pours two glasses of wine and grabs some chocolate to nibble on in the bed.

"I'm here and I can handle even this. Drink your wine and enjoy the chocolate. We need to call in the calvary." Before Sandy knew it, Jon was on the phone.

"Mary Ann, I need a little bit of help. Can you and Mildred try out the new elevator and come up to my office on the fourth floor? Yep, lock the front door and put the Be Right Back sign up."

Sandy looked at Jon like he was nuts. "What are you going to tell them and what do you think they are capable of?" she whispered.

Jon puts his finger to her lips. "Trust me. I'm not going to tell them your secret, well not the details at least. Watch and listen, they're amazing." Sandy was up, and had washed her face, combed her hair, and was sitting on the loveseat in Jon's new office. Sandy sips from the wine glass with plans to have more later. It was taking the edge off her nerves. And the chocolate, well chocolate just made everything better, right?

Another ten minutes later, all four are sitting around Jon's desk. Jon, Sandy, and Mildred were silent, but Mary Ann couldn't wait to find out the situation. "Okay, you in trouble little lady? And is Jon the cause of this trouble? Cause I know exactly what to do."

Jon burst out laughing and Mildred admonished Mary Ann for her crudeness. Sandy just rolled her eyes and put her face in her hands.

Jon said, "Well now, that's nonsense! Here's the problem. There are some people, not Texans or town folk but Italians, that may come looking for me or Miss McAllister. I need you two to sound the alarm if someone comes looking and keep them away from any knowledge of where she might be."

Mildred's eyebrows raise all the way to her hairline. "I love a good mystery and better yet to be in one. Sandy, both me and Mary Ann carry so we've got your back." Now it is Sandy's turn with the eyebrow thing, "You ladies are armed?"

"Yep and we're both pretty good shots. Our friend Lucy Mae can't hit a barn at three feet but she can scare the crap out of you when she's bellowing like a baby calf." Mary Ann is standing now and miming shooting from her hip. Mildred is just shaking her head.

This behavior didn't even phase Jon and he continued with his instructions. "I'd like it if you could call in your other wild women, including Lucy Mae, to take shifts manning the front desk here full time and the front desk at the hotel. It's not open, but there are workers in and out of there all day. I need to make sure that you know who comes and goes. Keep a log. Even take photos of everyone. It may be nothing, but we are going to be overly cautious and nosey about everyone, especially if they're not from here or new to the area."

"Does the sheriff know? What did he say? And you know full well that nosey is our middle name. What if someone doesn't want their photo taken?" With that announcement, Sandy couldn't contain a snicker.

Jon looked at Sandy and Mildred, maybe a little exasperated. "Mildred, first of all, if someone doesn't want their picture taken, do it anyway. That makes them a suspect. The sheriff will soon be looped in, but for now, trust no one. Not even Martha."

Mary Ann is up on her feet. "You suspect Martha? Well, I'll be…"

Jon was waving his hands for her to sit. "No, it was just a manner of speaking. I just don't want some stranger walking into the café and knowing all about Sandy and using it to hurt her.

So, can you keep this quiet?"

Mildred and Mary Ann stand and salute like good soldiers, and walk toward the elevator chatting about 'calling the girls,' making a schedule and other big plans, leaving Sandy and Jon alone.

"Well, that's our alarm system and it's worked in the past. I think it will help with this, too. We need to let Dylan, Owen, and Mike in on this right away."

Sandy tilted her head in confusion and Jon continued, "Owen Stone is a Texas ranger and his brother Mike, is a deputy sheriff and Dylan is the sheriff, all honest, trustworthy men." Sandy was not stupid enough to go at this alone and knew someone would be here as soon as her Dad got the message and sent out his style of alarm. Until then, she needed help because Pete and his guys were very good at making people disappear. Even with all of this, she was still worried.

Jon sees the worry on Sandy's face. "Let's get the second part of this plan in place."

Jon picked up the phone and called Sheriff Dylan Matthews. "Dylan, it's Jon over at the library. I'm calling an emergency meeting… Yeah, it's serious… I need you, Mike and Owen, as soon as possible… Well, right now. I'm on the fourth floor. I got the elevator fixed, so try it out. No guns needed yet, but definitely a notepad. Yep, that'll do."

"Guns?" Sandy had no other words. Jon sat next to her and moved her to his lap. Sandy snuggled in and holds on. This man was perfect. Once upon a time, Sandy had thought Pete was perfect, so maybe her sense of judgment was messed up. Oh hell, she decided she didn't care and snuggled even closer. She shivered and his arms around her tightened in response.

Jon's phone started to chirp and Sandy was sitting so close she could hear Mildred say Owen and Mike are on their way up. At that Sandy, could hear the elevator start its journey to them. Right before the doors opened from the elevator, Dylan appeared at the top of the stairs. "I win. I beat your new machine, Jon."

"Excuse me for interrupting, but I could have sworn you said you needed us now." Dylan was looking at Sandy and Jon tangled together on the little love seat. Jon narrowed his eyes. "Yes… Sandy needed some emotional support. Take a seat." From over by the elevator, Mike pipes in with, "I approve. That's my kind of support." All four men chuckle and Sandy blushes.

Jon didn't move a muscle, if anything he held on tighter, like a lion protecting his dinner as three others move in. Owen, who seems to be the oldest maybe, brings everyone back to the problem at hand. "Okay chief, what's up?"

Jon did move now and invited everyone to sit. "Sandy is in a fix and I think you all need to be aware of it and we need to have a plan of action." Jon quickly runs through what he knows about the problem with the skill of an experienced lawman. Sandy listens to these men hash out the issues and she realized that sitting before her was four lawmen not three. Owen keeps calling Jon, chief. What's all that about?

With Jon finished relaying what he knows, and the others supplying their opinions, all four sets of eyes land on Sandy. She had stayed silent so she could get a personal read on each one. These honest men looked ready to quiz her, or so she thought.

Owen turns back to Jon. "What kind of system for protection do you have in place? How can we help with that?"

"Sandy and I have Mildred, Mary Ann and their friends as the daytime alarm system and info collectors. I plan to fill in Martha later. She can be trusted, too. As for night hours, Sandy and I will work that out."

"Oh, I bet you will!" As soon as the naughty comment left Mike's mouth, a book whacked him upside of his head, courtesy of Owen. Everyone laughed, even Sandy.

Dylan, who had been quiet this whole time, finally spoke. "Sandy, tell us all you know about the others, besides Pete. Who else knows of you? Who is behind bars and who is not in that group? And tell us about Bob and your Dad."

Sandy took a deep breath, "my dad lives and works in Hagerstown, Maryland, and Bob is his best buddy from the Navy and he lives in Austin, Texas. Jaime is Bob's son and that is who allegedly called me, but I'm pretty sure it wasn't him. It just didn't sound like him and he did not ask the security question that was agreed upon. And most of all, he called me by my real first name. I'm so worried about Bob. I..."

Dylan holds up his hand and pulls out his phone, dials, and starts talking, "Jake, this is Sheriff Dylan Matthews, Somervell county in Twin Creeks, Texas. Badge number 35409. I need a well-check on a citizen in your jurisdiction... Yes, I do have that. Hold on." Sandy quickly writes down the info and hands it to Dylan. "Okay, ready? His name is Robert D. Manley of 9130 Balcones Club Drive. Austin... Thanks, call me back."

Dylan turns back. "I need info on your dad so I can do the same." Again, Sandy writes it down and Dylan makes the second call. When he's finished, Jon turned his computer screen around and he had pictures of Pete and some other old dudes up on the screen. "This is Gaitano Badalamante. He's serving time in federal prison, and this is his brother or maybe cousin, Salvatore Catalano, who is also incarcerated. The two younger men are Salvaltore's. Sal, a.k.a. Guy, and Pietro, a.k.a. Pete, Alfano, Gaitano's nephew. These two are the ones that Sandy is to testify against. The two in jail were part of the Pizza Connection case in the late eighties. These two took over just recently. They were raised in Sicily with family, and I do mean family."

There, next to the four men is a fifth picture of the agent who brought Pietro and Salvatore to justice and then jail. Sandy's mind finally makes the connection. "You're related to Irvin Wells, the man that headed the case against them back in the eighties? He's your ... I met your dad once, in Washington. And I remember now, he had flown in from Texas… Dallas, I think."

Owen, Mike, and Dylan all look at him with disbelief, but Owen finds his voice. "You didn't tell her? What's wrong with you? You being here is the key to this and is a big help."

"Wait, tell me what? Am I your job? Did my dad… Eww, or was it Bob who set this up?" Sandy was on her feet and heading for the elevator when Jon caught up. "Do I get the opportunity to explain?"

Sandy just stood silently, stiff as a board with her arms crossed, as the other three men drifted out, saying that they'd be back with intel soon.

Owen said, "Jon, stay here and keep her here. Even by force if you have to. Looks like you might have to. Good luck, Chief."

Jon just holds onto Sandy as they wait for privacy. She may be hurting inside, but she wasn't some young kid who wouldn't at least hear him out. That didn't mean she had to smile, but she would suck it up and listen. What had she missed? Could Dad and or Uncle Bob planned for her to meet him? Sandy is scolding herself about being too open and not careful.

Jon attempts to lead Sandy back to the love seat. "This may take a minute, so please sit." Sandy looks at this comfy sofa and does sit, not allowing him to join her. She couldn't have him that close. She knew she would fold and not even needing to listen to reason if this man was that close. Jon takes a step back and leans up against his desk.

"Okay, first, and most importantly, you are not my job. I did not know who you were until yesterday. I'm not sure what made me check on you through my sources, but when I realized who you were and how brave you were, I wanted to know you better. Honest. I went to Owen and he confirmed that he had visited with Bob when he was here buying the hotel. It all made sense. You've been hiding in plain sight. I just wasn't sure from what or who, at that time."

Sandy didn't say a word, her head was swimming with scary thoughts. She had done exactly what her dad and Bob had warned her not to do. She had allowed him into her close circle and allowed herself to be compromised by this beautiful, sexy man without even a thought of who he might be or what he might want. So stupid. Here she was, with strong feelings for this almost unknown man. She had even contemplated the existence of love at first sight with him. If this was not love at first sight, then she needed to start over and learn how to tell. She wanted, no needed, to be near him. Her mind wanders to him when they're apart, for heaven's sake. She even dreams about him. What was she going to do? Sandy's internal war is waging and she has no clue which argument is winning... the man she loved or the man who could have a not-so-nice agenda.

Jon waves his hand in front of her face and she bats him away, striking his arm hard. "Sorry, I didn't mean to hit you."

"Again, I am not so quick to let someone into

my private world just like you, so I chose not to be completely honest when I figured out how we were connected. Until I read your work, I had my doubts. Yes, my parents moved to the Dallas area, just like you, hiding in plain sight. Dad passed away six months ago and mom moved to Abilene with her sister. Dad didn't want us caught up in the mafia or whatever back then. Little did he know then that I'd grow up and be a part of the law enforcement family like him. When I was old enough, I went to the police academy. That was when he gave me his file and I read and reread it many times."

Sandy looked up at Jon leaving her inner thoughts behind. "Law Enforcement? You're the chief of police?"

Jon's rich laugh fills the room. "Hardly. I was a ranger like Owen is. I'm retired, due to an injury I suffered on the job as a Texas Ranger. We worked together for two years and yes, I was technically his superior, but we're only three years apart in age and two in service. We became good friends, as well as coworkers. Chief is a nickname I picked up along the way because I got along well with the Coushatta tribe in East Texas area near Livingston, Texas."

Jon's smile started to fail but he continues, "Every one of our conversations, I have been truthful, especially how I feel about you. I learned from that early experience, and Dad, to hold back all the details until needed. Today has happened so fast that I just haven't stopped to catch you up with how we fit together in history.

Owen knew about us because I needed to think about how to share my feelings with you and not have a situation where you didn't trust me. I clearly failed that big time. Owen's pissed I didn't tell you sooner. He was right. Because I drug my feet on this, I look like a dumb shit."

Sandy's head was spinning. Pete was on her trail. Dad had not called. Where was Bob? And even with all of that, this amazing man was still here, ready to love and care for her even in the face of evil. Sandy stood, stepped up close and kissed him. He immediately held on to her.

She leaned back. "After tonight, if you lie by omission to me you are going to regret it. There might be missing body parts. You've stolen my heart. I need you and want you... well, I've had you, but I want more time to have you again and again. So, don't mess up."

Jon's wolfish smile returns."Before we go to bed, emphasis on the bed, I'll tell you all you want to know." All of a sudden, Jon goes stock still, like a statue. He was so still that Sandy checked for a heartbeat. It was there, strong and steady... no, it was racing. "Are you ok, Jon? Your heart's going a mile a minute."

Without a word, Jon released her and went to the other side of the desk, opened a drawer, and pulls out a small bag. "Sandy, I'm not going to look like a dumb shit again because I waited too long to tell you how I feel. I know it's only been about five weeks but I believe in love at first sight."

Before Sandy could put two and two together,

he dropped to one knee. "Sandy McAllister, I was planning to do this in a very romantic place with music and friends. But it was in this office that I realized you're my kind of woman. You're different from any other woman I've dated, and more than anything else in this world I want to be a part of your life forever. Will you marry me? Wait, your real name is Kayleigh Sandra McAllister, right? I better be proposing to the right girl."

Sandy's lips part to speak, but she was stunned, relieved, excited, plus a million other emotions all wrapped into one, and so her brain stalled. This beautiful man was staring and waiting for a response. Sandy fights back tears. She hadn't known him long but love at first sight had crossed her mind, too... Several times. She'd dismissed it as wishful thinking but here it was on his mind, too.

Sandy looked into his eyes and could see into his soul. She placed her hands on his handsome, rugged face and gave him her answer. "Yes, you crazy, mixed up, beautiful man! I will marry you!" And then, she kissed him.

From across the room comes two squeals and clapping. Mildred's words rush out, "I know we should have let you know we were here, but we just were spellbound by the romantic moment. Forgive us... and congratulations! Welcome to the Twin Creek family."

No passionate kisses, well at least for the moment, but Sandy and Jon beamed. The elevator door opened and out walked Owen and

Dylan, carrying a file folder.

"I see you survived the explanation and she didn't maim you... Wait..." Owen's eyes drop to the ring. "You crazy fool. You did ask her? And she said yes? Damn, you are one slick operator, cause I know she isn't dumb."

Mike stepped up and shook Jon's hand and kissed Sandy on the cheek. "I guess this is as close as I'm going to get. Chief here has you all tied up in just over a month. Owen always said he was good, but until now I thought he was talking about being a lawman."

Dylan has the best observation. "Well Sandy, now you have a built-in bodyguard."

Sandy smiled. "You know Dylan, I do need a bodyguard and he is perfect. Plus, you should know that I might be a Yankee by birth, but I must have some Texan in me cause I'm a fair shot and do carry... So watch your p's and q's." Dylan doesn't even pause, "Dang and she's a feisty one, too. Just what you deserve, Jon."

Hugs and congratulations are passed around, then everyone sits down around Jon's desk to plan. The girl's report includes the name they have decided to call their gaggle of girlfriends. It's OHG, short for 'Over the Hill Girls'. Mildred hands out a schedule for the hotel and library front desks. At the top of the schedule the initials say OHG. Below OHG is a schedule of who and when, with phone numbers on it.

She proudly announces, "We start tomorrow. All these girls carry except one and she has a baseball bat that she's dang good with." All the men roll their eyes but Sandy answers. "Mildred, I'm so proud and want you to know that I'm pleased to be in the hands of the 'OHG.' You are the best alarm system money can't buy. But please be careful."

Mildred and Mary Ann are beaming and excuse themselves back to the front desk to close the library for the day. Jon's phone buzzes and the screen tells him it's Fred. Jon hands it over to Sandy. "Hey Fred… Yes, I know I haven't been around today… Yes, I'm at the library… Can you lock up and come on up to the fourth floor? Yes, Jon told me he bought the place and you helped him with the mysterious fourth floor… See you in a minute."

Owen nodded. "I think it's smart you tell Fred, but that means Eleanor will know and probably Jane, but I think that's okay. Besides, with the 'OHG' at the front desk, it would raise suspicion if you don't. Those ladies love to gossip, but not about safety and protection. I need to also speak with Martha."

Before Owen excused himself to find Martha, Fred arrived and is stunned into silence with the news of Sandy's story. "I thought you were hiding from maybe an over-possessive boyfriend or something. Never even crossed my mind it would be this dangerous, but I'm in. Where are you…" Fred spots the ring and looks from Jon to Sandy. He shakes his head. "I'm in so much trouble. Eleanor is… Well, I reckon I should get out the ring I bought a while back and make her an honest woman cause when she sees that ring and she doesn't have one of her own, I will be a dead man."

Sandy and Jon didn't say a word but Fred continues, "Okay, I know it's past due for me, but you two... I guess I should express my congratulations to the two of you and thank you for kicking this old man in the butt so I get on with tying the knot. You just made Eleanor's day. I guess I'll take her over to the café and let it be a spectacle. Hope you two join in. See you around seven?" Everyone nodded.

Fred was up and gone, and Sandy looked at Jon. "This is moving so fast. I want to savor it, but this threat is making me nervous." Dylan, Mike and Fred head out and wave goodbye.

Jon was up and moving to his apartment with Sandy by the hand as soon as the men disappeared down the stairs. "Come on, let's get a snack to hold us over until we go to the café for the spectacle at seven."

EIGHT

SANDY WAS BEGINNING TO SEE both sides of a small town, the good and the not so good. Everyone knew about her engagement to Jon and expressed their excitement. That was the scary part. She loved that they cared, but that much talk was bound to bring nosey outsiders into the mix. She just prayed she never found Pete at her front door. Dad and Bob had drilled into her head that news like that traveled fast. Pete had a powerful family behind him and more than enough money to buy anyone. He had made bail with the help of some very powerful and influential lawyers back east. There were restrictions to his travel, but when the case moved from Virginia to Dallas, things changed. This meant Pete's family would get in touch with their contacts here in Texas. That would allow him to roam free in this big state, too close to her. Sandy told Jon about her fears… Pete being so close. Jon immediately relayed that news to Owen.

The OHG was diligent with photos, news and names. It was nice having someone at the front desk and Sandy planned to keep this in place when she opened. She wanted to pay the ladies, but none would think of it. Once she opened, she would change that arrangement but for now, it was a battle for another day.

Sandys favorite OHG was Rosalie. She wields a mean baseball bat. As the story goes, she was the best hitter, amongst girls and boys, at the high school. To hear Rosalie, she's still the best hitter because there's no one brave enough to challenge her. Rosalie is a widow with a zillion grandkids. A different one brings her lunch every day. Her shift is from seven till noon. When she finishes her shift, she and whichever grandkid arrives with lunch eat together on the porch, or in the dining room, if the weather is bad.

Rosalie is full of stories of the hotel and how she longed to stay here. She said, "This hotel was the finest place around. I'm so glad to see it back." Sandy listens. Rosalie's tales would add charm when Sandy had the place open, even if she was just sitting on the porch as a greeter. Rosalie, at eighty-four, remembers the last owner of the place. Sandy sits down at the table to listen Rosalie share what she remembers. "Well, little lady... That sweet Maybelline, she was the owner, wanted Sarah and Mitchel Forester to come take the place over before she died, but somehow that didn't happen. Maybelline was just going to give it to them. Maybelline thought it was all arranged for them to come here with their new baby girl that summer of 2007. Mitchel Forester was from Utah and Sarah was distantly related to Maybelline. They were supposedly on their way from his parents' home in Utah. They never came and she passed in August of 2007. The hotel hadn't been busy, so it closed and that was that."

Sandy asked questions about the will and who got what, but Rosalie just didn't know or didn't remember. Michael, the twelve-year-old grandson visiting that day, said, "I'll ask my mom if she remembers anything. My mom knows everything." Sandy thanked him and hoped he would remember to talk to his mom.

Two nights later, Sandy was telling Jon about how she hoped Rosalie would continue to be at the B&B during the day and that she remembered the last owner of the hotel. Jon loved the idea of her being the greeter. He suggested that since Rosalie wouldn't take payment, Sandy should just open an account so that she could stop at Martha's and have dinner on Sandy. Sandy loved that idea and would make those arrangements when the time came. They were sitting in his bed, watching the sunset. "I never get tired of this. It makes me thankful that I've made it through another day with you and still want more." Jon's words were exactly how Sandy was feeling, too. "Yes, I feel the same. I never get tired of being with you. Do you really think it's necessary that we sleep at both of our places with no particular schedule?"

Jon keeps looking straight at the sunset when he answers. "A pattern in your schedule is a good way to be caught off guard and it's the first thing you look at to confront or capture someone. Noticing when you're alone is the second thing to watch for, neither of those two things are going to catch us unaware. Last night and tonight, we're here. Tomorrow, we will be at your place. By then, Fred will have installed some cameras and sensors for at night in both places."

The B&B wasn't empty because Eleanor went and set up a bed in one of the three bedrooms behind the kitchen. Fred and Eleanor will stay at the B&B for the time being. Fred was happy to be close to his work and Eleanor enjoyed all the action and getting to be so close to Fred all day. Rocky's friend, Madeleine, wouldn't be back until New Year's Eve. Mike and Dylan's group added both buildings and the shared alley into their patrols at night. Both Sandy and Jon were lost in their thoughts when Jon broke the silence. "When I revamped this floor, I added security cameras on the first floor and up here. I ordered more cameras for the other floors and they just arrived. One of Fred's guys and I will install them tomorrow."

Sandy put her hand on Jon's arm. "Thanks to you, I know Dylan got the well-check report back on my dad and he's fine. And Jaime didn't make the call to me because he was on some cruise with his new girlfriend. So, I know you're on top of things? But what about Bob. I'm so worried."

Before Jon could answer Sandy, his phone rings. Sandy could see anxiety in his eyes. "Hello? Speaking. Holy cow, that's great!" Jon puts his thumbs up. "When? Where? How bad?

Thanks, I'll pass the info along."

Sandy was almost out of control when he finally hung up. "Okay spill. Was that about Bob? Is he okay? Where is he?"

Jon turns and holds her. "You're right, it was about Bob. He's been located alive but in bad shape in a tiny hospital in Marble Falls, Texas. Your dad is there now. You should get a text from your dad soon on your burner phone. Someone tried to kill Bob for info on you, but Bob escaped even though he took a beating. Bob made it to Marble Falls from Austin to a friend's house, and then into a hospital there under an fake name. The friend called your dad. Your dad was already on the move because of your email so when he heard from Bob's friend, he made arrangements for Bob to be airlifted to Lackland Air Force hospital in San Antonio. He'll make it."

Sandy's relief came in the form of tears that soon turned into sobs. She lay there sobbing in Jon's arms until she slept. Jon got up and double-checked all the locks and alarms and cameras, plus put in a call to Dylan, Mike and Owen with the news about Bob.

He hoped the additional cameras and the police scheduled rounds would be enough. He joined Sandy, knowing that tomorrow will bring new challenges. For his beautiful soulmate, he was ready and willing.

Sandy opened her eyes and spent the first few minutes of waking up just taking Jon in. Not only was he handsome and a thorough, dedicated lover, he was a wonderful man through and through. His loving manner made Sandy crave to be in his presence and his sharp mind made her respect him more.

When she rolls over and pulls the covers up, she sees that the weather had turned nasty. It seemed to have snowed again last night and it sounded like it was sleeting. Good thing all her work today was scheduled to be inside so she'd be warm and cozy. The clock on the side table read six-thirty a.m. Mildred was on duty this morning, and she and Mary Ann should arrive soon to begin their morning ritual of making coffee and enjoying treats from the Cynfully Delicious Bakery on the square.

Jon was lightly snoring and cuddled up closer to her. His hands were searching, then caressing her. She returned the favor and his eyes popped open as her hands explored his growing manhood. He made a growling noise deep in his throat as he started to wake. "I love waking up to your soft touches, but I'm in the mood for something a little rougher, lady." Jon moved Sandy, intending to sit her in his lap, just as there were multiple pings from the security cameras. "Shit, if that's that cat walking on the fire escape again, I…" With his phone in his hand, both can see a strange figure just inside the front door trying to open the door to the stairs that come up to his place. This wasn't good.

Jon and Sandy quietly and quickly dress in warm clothes. Jon was keeping an eye on the screen and what was happening downstairs. Jon has a double lock on the door from here to the first floor, but the one at the bottom was not as secure as it would be by the end of today. He pushed a dresser in front of one door and a bookcase in front of the other. Sandy is dressed, has her revolver in hand, and is still watching the man pick the lock. The man trying to break in stops and talks to someone out of the camera's view and then continues on when he hears the furniture moving. Jon was on the phone and calling for help.

"Come on. Help is on the way, but we're not going to wait around. Who knows how many there might be." With that, Jon and Sandy pull on sweatshirts, gloves and boots so that being outside would at least be tolerable. Jon changes screens on Sandy's phone to the cameras in his office on the fourth floor.

Sandy whispers, "Is someone out there?" He must see someone or something, because he motions for Sandy to retreat. Ever so carefully, he pushes a second bookcase against it. The window in his bathroom had access to the fire escape. Jon has his gun drawn and waves Sandy to the bathroom. Once inside, Sandy climbs onto the toilet, opens the window and moves out onto the fire escape, despite the bitter cold she was met with. The wind was brutal and the sleet hurt as it pelts her in face. Jon was right behind her, but that didn't quell her fear.

Through the window, both can hear a woman scream, then a second. Oh God, that has to be Mary Ann or Mildred. Sandy was frightened for herself, but more so for them. Lights go on in her B&B, but Jon waves to keep moving. The rails are cold and slippery from the raging storm. Jon points to the man just getting on the fire escape below. "Go up and hurry. We can use the ladder to cross. Come on Sandy, I know you don't like this but move."

He was right, Sandy was terrified. She was moving but it was slick and she wished she had on tennis shoes and not these boots. The boots were warm but they tended to slip. Sandy reached the top and so did Jon. He went to the crank to swing the ladder across while Sandy took off her boots and threw them at a man below. The first missed him, but the second one hit him square in the head which sent him to the ground and he lost his gun.

When his gun hit the ground, it discharged. It was like a cannon going off in the small area of the alley and would bring a crowd, even in this weather. That bit of commotion had given Jon and Sandy enough time to get on the ladder walkway and make it more than halfway across when another shot rang out. This one hit the roof of Sandy's building, missing them by inches. Jon turned and fired back. Both heard a grunt and a thud, and she hoped it had at least disabled their pursuer. Shouts are heard from down below as Sandy and Jon scurry on. Voices call out instructions, where they are and who they have. The bad guy on the first part of the fire escape jumped to the ground and was running away.

Owen's distinctive voice rang out. "I got one

handcuffed and this one here in the bathroom is shot and not going anywhere fast." Sandy looked up to climb onto the roof of her building when she was roughly grabbed. Her reflexes make her pull away but she soon saw it was Fred. His face was so worried and relieved all at once. "Come here child, quickly."

Sandy was more than happy to comply. She kind of leaped into Fred's arms. Safety, at last! Fred took the revolver from her hand and backed her inside the building. Jon turned back to help contain the injured man, find out who had screamed, and secure his building.

An hour, and several mugs of cocoa, later, everyone was sitting around the biggest table in the café. The café was closed, but this was a private meeting. As townies arrive for breakfast, Martha lets them in with a whispered message. All was quiet. Owen was definitely in charge and was fielding most of the questions. "Everyone, hold on with the questions for a minute. I'll tell you what I know." He cleared his throat and began, "We're pretty sure there were four men, might have been a driver waiting for them over behind the old mill. We're just not sure yet. We have three of them locked up. I've called for help to take them out of here and over to Dallas to the Feds. I worry that one for sure, and maybe two, got away. They'll be back."

Sandy was so cold after her climb across the building. Fred had kept her wrapped in a blanket, hidden under the stairwell with her gun until the all-clear message was sent. Sandy hadn't seen

Jon since he turned back to help. Owen spoke as if he had read her mind, "Jon should be here in a minute." He looked past all of them and pointed. "Looks like he's coming now with his posse."

The door opens and a strong cold wind blows in with Jon, Mildred, and Mary Ann. Jon hands Owen a phone with a purple case, definitely not his color. "Owen, Mildred has a picture of the whole group, all five. She managed to get it right before they locked her and Mary Ann in the supply closet. She also recorded what they said to each other right before they went upstairs to take out Sandy and whoever else that got in the way."

The room went dead still as everyone listened to the recording. "Split up. You have your assignments. Mac, to the fire escape. Bill, go get the car. This shouldn't take long. The three of us will head up to the fourth floor and get this done. Pete wants her if we can capture her alive. If not, then dead." The room is silent as everyone took in the eerie, cold-hearted conversation.

Jon walked straight to Sandy and scooped her into his arms. He whispered into her hair, "I'm so glad all is okay with you. I was so scared for you." Jon turned to Fred, "I want to thank you for being there for Sandy. She's my everything." Fred grinned, "She's important to me, as well. I'm just glad the call went out."

In the small silence, while most are watching Jon and Sandy's reunion, Mildred is still in her fighting mood. "Those slimy 'eye-talian' gangsters are going to get more than they ever dreamed of if they show their faces here again." Most of the folks in the café agree with Mildred.

Owen's big voice took over again. "People, we have a problem, those sorry excuses for humans will be back. They didn't get what they came for. I think we should all get some rest and meet here, about one. By then, we'll have given the three we have to the FBI and will have some idea of what to do next. If you have ideas, I want to hear them. Good night, everyone. Well, morning, I guess. Don't go home alone. There are two still on the loose."

Jon speaks up, "There was blood where the getaway car was parked, so most likely one is injured. Dylan issued a BOLO on the remaining two, and sent out these pictures. Everyone, please be careful. These were all hired professionals, doing the main guys' dirty work. Mildred will be sending all of you a picture of Pete and his cousin Guy, short for Giuseppe, plus the other pictures she has. Be careful."

Fred, Eleanor, Sandy, and Jon all start across the courthouse lawn. The sleet has stopped and the roads are slippery but passable. Mildred and Mary Ann are in pickup trucks with men that must be their husbands. Everyone looks and sounds tired. With the adrenalin rush gone, so is their strength. Eleanor looked up into a now clear sky at the North Star disappearing as the day is beginning. "Look at that star, will ya? It's leading us straight to bed." Everyone laughed and Fred has the door unlocked and open when Jon notices the camera blinking. Everyone else follows his line of sight. Fred heads straight to the closet where the equipment was that was monitoring the place. Jon had forgotten all about the cameras in the craziness of the early morning. He was on the phone and minutes later Owen, Dylan, and Mike were all squished into the storage closet with Sandy, Eleanor, Fred and Jon, watching the film that shows two men casing the place.

They were different men from the ones that Mildred had captured in her photos. One man comes clearly into sight and Sandy gasps, "Oh my God, that's Pete. Oh no, he's found me." The tears are non-stop. Jon extracts Sandy from the closet and is just about to take her upstairs when Dylan popped out of the closet and says quietly, "Jon… No." With very few words and a lot of hand gestures, Sandy was back in the closet with Eleanor, with orders to stay put. All five men have their guns drawn. After clearing the first floor, Fred stood by the closet door ready to shoot.

Moving as a disciplined team, the four lawmen go up the stairs. Twenty scary minutes later, they were back to the first floor and Fred was letting two people in the front door. Owen speaks as he made his way down from the second-floor landing to the entry. "Howdy, Agent Martin. That's Sandy and this is her place. We've just secured the building. Thank you for the offer of walking through both places to check for cameras or any other devices. We don't have much need for that technology training here in

Twin Creeks."

With a quick smile, Agent Martin nods at Sandy. "Nice to meet you. I talked to your dad earlier and apprised him of the situation. This is Agent MacNamara, she will do the device check." Before he could continue, Mike steps up, "I'll be glad to take you through the place. If that's okay?"

Agent Martin nods, and Mike and Agent MacNamara start in the kitchen. "As soon as this room is clear, I need you to bring me up to present on what is happening here now and this morning's tense moments. I want to have a copy of the footage from here and your place, Jon."

Eleanor is at the kitchen door and invites everyone in for coffee and pancakes.

"Something smells awful good in here." Comes from Mike, as he and Agent MacNamara finish scanning for devices in the kitchen. "We'll be back for our pancakes in ten minutes or less."

Ten minutes later and with pancakes in front of them, Agent MacNamara began her to report about what she found.

"There are four audio bugs in the place. Two on the fourth floor, one in the elevator and one out in the library. I turned music on in the fourth floor and library for camouflage for now. Elevator is up and running, so be careful."

There was much discussion about what to do. Finally, it was decided to leave the one in the library there and jam it on and off as needed to feed false info to the listeners, but remove the others noisily so they hear them getting found.

Owen likes this idea. "So that means we talk in the library to feed them info we want them to know. We need our first info session to be about what we found and that we're sure we found them all and later hold scripted meetings in there."

Agent Martin nodded. "You need to be aware that they will make their move sooner rather than later because the trial was moved up to mid-January. If my info is correct, the trial is set for January seventh. I had already been asked to come and meet with you, Sandy, before this attempt today. I wish I had come sooner."

Sandy had been picking at her food and Jon had been watching her. She was quiet, like a bomb ready to explode. He could feel the pressure building. He moved his chair closer. In her hair, he whispered, "Let's go to your room for a while so we can talk." She doesn't answer but does push her chair back and then stops. "Did you take the bugs from my room yet?"

Agent MacNamara was up and moving, "I can do that right now. Mike can you help me discover them. Just follow my lead. Be back in a jiffy. Let's have that meeting for the bad guys to hear in the library in five minutes. I will come in triumphant with my finds. Please react accordingly." Mike nods and adds, "Let's get the elevator first, then the two in Sandy's place."

True to her word, they were back in record time and triumphant. The acting was Oscar-quality, but all Sandy wanted was a safe place to be.

NINE

FOUR HOURS LATER, A CROWD of fifty or so townies were seated and back to talking softly in the café, waiting for Owen to begin his briefing. "Thank you all for being here. Thank you for writing your questions on the café's chalk board, that way I can answer them all. During the meeting, if you think of a question I haven't answered, write it down and Vanessa will come get it so I can be thorough."

Dylan stands and announces, "If anyone else wants to be on the text alert group, put your name and number on the paper coming around. Please silence your phones during the meeting, because your phone will be receiving pics of the bad guys while Owen is talking. Thanks."

Mike hands out the papers, and Martha and Vanessa are taking orders and delivering coffee to all who want it. Cynfully Delicious Bakery had sent boxes of goodies. Owen moves back to the front, "the first thing I want to make clear is that you absolutely do not approach these people. Do not trust anyone you have not met before. If there is a stranger, text or call for help, even if you think they're harmless. Do not be alone with them. If you need to send them anywhere, send them to the library. Then, text immediately to the number I've given you. Safety comes first. Those of you who are here just to be informed and don't wish to be involved any further, that's okay and actually recommended. Leave town, go visit family for the rest of the holidays or just lay low. This situation shouldn't go beyond January seventh."

Several people got up and left. One stops and looks back, "I wish you all luck and I pray this is over safely and soon. I'll be taking my family for a short trip to visit relatives and friends, but will watch the updates."

After the door closes, Owen begins again. "This is voluntary. Never put yourself in danger, that's what we're here for. If you have security cameras, make sure they're on and working; we may need them. It's that old saying… If you see something, say something… You will always find someone to help you on the fourth floor of the library. The people there are ready and willing to help or just listen. We've been feeding false info through a bug that they left planted in the library of the McCormick B&B. If you find yourself there, be careful what you say. For now, we're talking into that bug about a New Year's Eve fireworks display, to happen out at the auction barn with a party afterward. Also, Sandy has said to the bug with Jane there to thank her dad but she will be with Jon in the library New Year's Eve. Sandy also fed false intel that Jon and Her would be on the roof watching the fireworks from there. Our bad guys that are listening will hopefully think everyone is out of the town center. We need a big crowd to make this work. Sandy is catering, with the help of Martha and Cynthia and it is all free to the townsfolks. Please RSVP to Martha or Cynthia. Bring your own drinks, lawn chairs and blankets. There is a bonfire arranged, too. This should be a lovely evening for the family. So, please help by coming."

Mike steps up next to Owen. "I'm in charge of surveillance, so if you have a camera please see me after this with its location so I can see where our dead spots are. If you have a camera but you're not sure if it works, I can help. If you have a camera but it's still in the box, I want to hear from you as well. We can install it with your help. If you want to buy a camera, come see me, too."

Dylan ends the meeting with, "I'm sticking close the Sheriff's office, Fred will be at the B&B, Mike will be on the move and Owen and Jon will be on the fourth floor of the library most of the time if you need one of us."

Sandy was so grateful for all this support. No matter if it was hands-on or just going to the fireworks viewing party, both would help. Jon had come back to her table and had all kinds of papers to sort. "Sandy, let's go to my office. I'm sure that most of the work that needed to be done here is finished. I can finish this paperwork and keep you close." Jon and Sandy were up and off to the library before most of the crowd dispersed.

It was breezy out, but much warmer than last night, and not a cloud in the sky. Jon could see the tension and anxiety all over Sandy. "This lovely, mild weather is supposed to hold until after the first." Sandy took a deep breath and realized it was a beautiful day, weather-wise. It wasn't warm, but rather unseasonably mild for late December. Her head was filled with worry but one of her favorite teachers said to her when her mother had passed, "Live life like today is your last. It may be all you get. Your mom did that and she would want you to do that, too." That teacher had helped with those words more than she would ever know. Teachers were amazing, they give and give and give in hopes that one day their words would be there to help. Mission accomplished, Mrs. Magill. I heard you.

Jon stops dead in his tracks and Sandy takes two steps before she realized he stopped. "What is it?"

"It's you. I need you to be present. You're a million miles away and that can't happen right now. Stay with me."

Sandy knew he was right, so she grabbed his elbow, and started forward. "I'll do better. I know I need to be with you in the present. Getting lost in the past isn't going to help me."

Jon pointed out cameras as they walked. She could see the new ones at the library as they approached. Jon opened the door for her and a doorbell noise went off as they stepped in.

Sandy startles at this new surprise. "That's new." Mary Ann's voice rings out from somewhere, "I love that I can see who comes in without being right there. This is amazing!" Mildred's voice was next. "You're supposed to have the mute button on, you old coot, or you just broadcast to the whole building like we're doing right now."

Jon laughed. "Some security system when the caretakers can't work it."

Again, Jon and Sandy overhear their little squabble. "Here's the mute button." Then, "I know, I see it. I've got this." And back to Mildred, "Then why don't you d—" And then their voices cut off.

Sandy looked at Jon. "Well, I guess that's fixed."

On the fourth floor, things have changed. Seated and busy at computers are three people Sandy has never seen before. As Sandy and Jon arrived, they all stood and came to Jon's desk and waited. Sandy started to introduce herself when the older woman said, "no need, Ms. McAllister. We know who you are, Owen briefed us. There will be a team of three here at all times. We're the technicians, here to make sure all of the surveillance equipment is working. The first real tactical team should be here any minute and we'll show them, and you two, what's here. Then we'll depart to our next assignment. We're not finished just yet, so excuse us for now."

Jon thanked them and waved them off. "Come on Sandy, let's get a drink. I have new locks in the apartment to show you." Sandy watched as Jon unlocks the deadbolt to his apartment. An alarm immediately sounds.

Sandy stepped closer. "Why is that going off? Is someone breaking in?" Her voice is shaking and Jon understands he's made a mistake showing her and not telling her first about it. The alarm has frightened her unnecessarily.

Jon moved closer and holds her. "I'm so sorry. I never thought about the alarm possibly spooking you. If you put the key in, but don't punch in the code, the alarm will go off. If you turn the knob while it's locked from the outside, it will go off." While Jon was explaining, one of the techs had stopped the noise and sent an all-clear text to the others.

The older woman was in his face. "Not only did you scare Ms. McAllister to death, that alarm will bring everyone with guns drawn. Be careful not to cry wolf."

Jon was scratching his head and apologized to everyone. "I didn't know it was hooked up to the team yet.

"Well, ask. What do you think we are doing here? You need to stay in the present if you're going to protect her." Sandy couldn't help the smile that crossed her face, but she covered it by looking down and away. These were the words he had just scolded her with on their walk to the library. Can you say karma?

Seconds later, Mike popped out of the elevator. "Is it really a false alarm? I was on my way here anyway when I heard the alarm, then I got the all-clear. What's up?"

Sandy could see Jon was not happy with

himself. "Jon was showing me the safety features here and inadvertently set off the door alarm. I guess I need to know more because I could easily do that, too."

Mike came closer to the tech group. "Looks like this is almost done. I need a tour of this stuff. You two go on, I'm going to stay right here and learn."

Jon turned and was muttering under his breath, "I know exactly what kind of equipment he'll be examining." Sandy followed him into the apartment and immediately noticed that even though the windows still had blinds and drapes, they seemed darker somehow. Sandy watched as Jon made his way to the fridge. "What changed with the windows? Somehow they look darker."

Jon grabbed a drink and turned. "I had them tinted dark. The summers here are so bright that the sun would have heated this place up like an oven. That sunset is beautiful, but with its slow decent, this part of the building will heat up quickly. It won't do that so much now, but in the summer it will. It also makes it very difficult to see in from the outside. I had planned to wait until later this year to do it, but when I called about it the guy said he could do it now and for much cheaper since he wasn't busy. Win, win. Maybe you should think about your window seat and the honeymoon suite windows."

Sandy nodded and wandered over to the sofa and sat heavily on it, kicking her boots off and putting her feet up. She yawned and then closed her eyes. Jon came close. "Why don't you stretch out on the bed? You have to be exhausted. Nothing more important is happening that you need to be around for. I got this."

With that Sandy stood and went straight to bed. She did need some sleep.

TEN

WITH THREE DAYS TO GET the New Year's Eve celebration at the auction house arranged and everyone on board, and have supplies delivered on time, Sandy was going to be seriously busy. Not to mention, the numerous interruptions for conversations in the small library of the hotel to feed fake information to the bad guys bug. Each night, Sandy just fell into bed and slept. Jon wasn't having such an easy time relaxing into sleep. At night, he would sit next to Sandy in bed until he knew she was asleep and then he'd recheck the security measures that were now in place. He hated this part of any operation. Waiting for the plan to start, rethinking all the safeguards, wondering if there was something else that should be done.

Sandy plans on spending the twenty-ninth and thirtieth at the auction barn working on the party. This is one party she wished she'd be at. Instead, she'd be locked up in the library on the fourth floor with a beautiful man she adored. Well, both places would be fun, but the library would be stressful, like sitting ducks waiting to be shot at.

Jon had told her about the evening plans. Everything seemed to be ready. Sandy was sitting there, half listening to the chatter in Jon's office. Jon leaned into her, "listen for a minute, then you and I will go over to your place and finalize the plans for the bug." Sandy knew that today was for finishing the plans for the fireworks guys, to begin with the delivery of the fireworks and get a timeline in place for the party. They said that they would have the setup done by four-thirty on the day-of. Dark was around six and it should be clear enough to see every star in the sky. Perfect. The first display should run around ten to fifteen minutes for the young kids. The fireworks would be set off by George Gilroy's brother, Sam, around seven. The band was scheduled to start right after it in the big barn. The bonfire would be ready for s'mores by seven, too. The local Boy Scout troop was to be in charge of it. Food should start at five or so, with a big buffet in the barn for snacks and munchies. There should be something for everyone. A second, larger fireworks display was scheduled for a few seconds before midnight. It should last twenty to thirty minutes.

All the good guys were here. Sandy almost felt like this could be a planning meeting for any big party. But she knows all too well, the bad guys were dangerous, with a capital D for deadly. Jon handed everyone a schedule. "This is the schedule and who is in charge of each activity. Sandy and I will talk about going to the party later this evening in front of the bug, but then ultimately decide to stay in. Fred, Eleanor, and Jane, you have parts to play so be in the hotel kitchen by seven-thirty. Hopefully, all this chatter about 'outsiders being hired to work at the party so the town folks will enjoy a work-free party to end the old year and bring in a wonderful new year' will ring true enough to the bad guys. These arrangements will be good cover for all the law enforcement folks being brought in that day."

Sandy stood and waited for everyone to quiet down. "I just want to thank all of you. I can't explain how I feel about your willingness to help me. I know the law enforcement crowd will say it is their job, but I'm glad you're here. And the citizens of Twin Creeks, I'm so sorry I brought this threat to you. I started to pack up and leave, but I've been made to realize that anywhere I go, I will put someone in danger. Thank you again for adopting me as part of the Twin Creeks family"

Friendly smiles along with sympathetic ones were exchanged and the team was back to work. Jon handed Sandy the script for later. This was so important to get it right and come off as believable.

Sandy read through the script for this evening. She wanted to bait the trap perfectly so this could be done and over with. Her real phone had not been turned on since the call from the fake Jaime so all she had was the burner phone and it didn't have very many prepaid minutes on it. This phone was for her dad. There was commotion all around her but she was lost in her thoughts when Mike sat down beside her. "Here, you need this. I had your old phone number changed and had the techs here look at it and make sure it was sheltered as much as possible so we can alert you and also track you quickly. Jon, Owen, Dylan, and I have the app that does that and only us. When all this is over, I can fix it so you aren't tracked anymore."

There was a new appreciation for this man's talents and it was not just his ability to charm all the females around. Sandy smiled and hugged him, with a thank you kiss on the cheek. Mike, the ever-present flirt, turned his head just in time for her to plant that kiss on his lips, not his cheek. Sandy was surprised and Mike claps. "Got ya!" With that, Jon helped him out of the seat next to Sandy with a grunt. "Just you wait 'til you have your own special girl about and I'm obnoxious like you are now. We'll see how you like it then."

This commotion stopped everyone, kind of like a pause button on Netflix, but when Mike hit the hard seat next to the sofa, the play button was pressed and the commotion began again just where it left off. Sandy couldn't help but smile at Jon's cute jealousy. The afternoon wore on and people came and went. If there was something not planned, Sandy couldn't think of what it could be. The only variable now was if Pete and all his men would fall into their plans.

Jon and Sandy left the comfort of the fourth-floor office and apartment to check on the hotel and Fred's work. Sandy knew the work was complete in the first two rooms on the second floor and hoped that the honeymoon suite was ready for décor. This was so exciting. Seeing something normal go on would be nice.

Fred sat down at the kitchen table. "Sandy, before we talk about the second floor, I wanted to talk to you about the three rooms on the first floor behind the kitchen. I know you have planned on waiting to do any real work there for a while. I just have a few questions about the first-floor design."

The first-floor bedrooms were not even something that Sandy had thought about in days. But Fred unrolls the floor plan and begins. "We need a better restroom on the first floor for the general public. There's a butler's pantry attached to the dining room and I want to put it there. Then the storage closet behind it, it opens into the hall behind the kitchen where the three rooms are could be changed to a small shower/ restroom for the first room behind the kitchen. There's plumbing running close to it in the basement and it won't add much to the overall budget. That means the other two rooms can be opened up to make a good size room with a seating area and its own bathroom. This is getting the best bang for your buck."

Sandy stared at him for a silent moment then looked up. "You've added to my plans and improved it so much. I love that idea!"

Fred let out a long breath and Eleanor claps. "I knew she would love it."

Fred still seemed disturbed, or was he anxious? "Okay, Sandy. It's true confession time. As you know, Eleanor and I have been staying here so I can work and still be close to her and the action and help."

"Yes Fred, I know that and I'm grateful for your help with everything. So, what's wrong and why do you need to confess?"

"Well hell, come on. I'll show you." Fred was up and heading for the hallway behind the kitchen. Sandy, Jon, and Eleanor followed him. Sandy could see that where the door to the storage room opened to the hall was gone. Fred opens the first room door and stepped aside. Sandy entered and realized this room was where she stayed those first few days but it was completely different. The storage room opened with a sliding barn door to reveal an ultra-modern bathroom with old-timey looking fixtures. The room was painted a soft yellow and had simple white sheets on the bed. It was beautiful.

Sandy managed to find words, "This is amazing. How... When did you get this done? No, never mind that, how much did this cost? No... I don't care. It's better than I had planned. Thank you."

Eleanor giggled. "If she likes this, then I know she will like the rest."

"Rest? What rest?" Sandy started to mirror some of Fred's anxiety.

Eleanor didn't notice Fred's grimace. She just took Sandy by the hand and led her across the hall. There used to be two doors on that side of the hall, but now there was just one big, oversized door and a full-length antique mirror approximately where the other door had been.

"Look at this! Isn't it stunning? It needs a name and your designer's touch."

Sandy stood stock still and just took it all in. Fred interrupted the silence. "Eleanor and I work on it every night. It's our gift to you. This job, working for you, has put both of us in a good place financially and romantically. We are so grateful."

Sandy could not wrap her brain around the lovely space. Jon stepped up behind her and pulled her close. "It's really nice, don't you think?"

Sandy sputtered to life. "Oh yes... I mean, again it is so much better than my plans. How did you two do this without me noticing? I guess my mind has been other places, as well as my body, these past days. It's beautiful."

Eleanor crowded past Jon and Sandy. "This was fun. Jane helped paint and sand the foor, shift furniture around. Fred took care of cleaning the windows and the replacing the bathroom fixtures. This place has good bones. The little loveseat, chair and bedroom furniture are on loan from the auction house. You can choose to buy them or not."

Jane popped in from the kitchen. "Sorry I'm late. I heard you talking about me just now. I hope it was good."

Leave it to Jane to break the tension. Sandy was still silent and was very aware that everyone was waiting for her. "I'm not talking 'cause I'm just stunned with what you have done, and behind my back no less. It's amazing... I love it all."

Jane laughs. "Are you kidding? We could have paraded an elephant in here, right by your nose and you wouldn't have noticed. Your brain has been somewhere else." No one laughed, but Sandy knew they wanted to, so she did.

Sandy grabbed Jane and gave her a noogie. "You're absolutely right, I have had my head in the clouds. That will change right now. Let's go get our lines down and feed fake info to the bad guys."

Thirty minutes later, they all felt comfortable enough to get the fake news done. Their practice time caused a lot of laughs and funny moments to ease the tension of the seriousness at hand. Everyone went to their places. Jon checked the front door. It was locked, and had a sign up saying to check back in thirty minutes.

The hardest thing was not to giggle at the big sign above the recording device. It was a picture of a bug with an arrow pointing at it. Jane had owned up to the drawing but Fred had hung it. It was a silly cartoon of a bug with big ears attached. The sign was impossible to miss.

Jon went to the jamming device and slowly turned the music off so their words could be heard. Eleanor had been charged to turn it off and on four or five times a day and put on soft music all night so they would listen. This little thing was the key to the whole plan. Jon whispered to Sandy, "Here goes nothing. Well, really, here goes everything."

Jon began the scene. "Hey Sandy, can you come here? Bring Eleanor with you."

In the distance, you can hear Sandy shout, "Coming. Give me a minute."

Sandy and Eleanor enter the library together, giggling. Jon asks, "What's so funny?"

Eleanor responded, "Just girl talk. What do you need? I'm cleaning up dinner and have bread for tomorrow in the oven."

"Can you make it quick, we have so much to do before the big celebration tomorrow night. Eleanor and I will be up all night getting it done," Sandy added.

"Fred and I have been going over the plans and we're worried those men will return for you so we don't think you should go to the party. You will be too exposed and so will the others."

"What? Not go at all? Eleanor raises her voice. Sandy shushes her,

"Jon has a point. Maybe I should just stay here alone. I can lock myself in and read a book and watch the fireworks from the big window at Jon's place. My window seat is kinda small, but his window is huge."

Jane enters the room making a lot of noise trying to practice her flute. Eleanor is the first to get to her at the door. "Hush girl, we're trying to have a meeting."

Jane moves farther in the room, "Did I hear Sandy say she wasn't going to go to the New Year's Eve Party? Cause that's crazy."

Sandy signals to Jane. "Come over and join

the meeting. It's a plan, not a secret meeting, so help us with the plan. I'm just trying to think of others. Everyone here has responsibilities except me, so I won't be missed. I will still be at the brunch on the first. I'm sure Jon will check on me after the fireworks go off. He can't come before that because he's in charge of them."

"No, no, no, that's not fair. I want you to come. Everyone in the county will be at this party. I mean Twin Creeks will be like a western ghost town."

Fred puts his arm around Jane, "Settle down, Jane. We will make sure Sandy has food and can easily see the fireworks from Jon's place. He'll come and check on her after midnight."

"Yea, Jane. It's about a twenty-minute drive from your uncle's auction house so I should arrive to check on Sandy a few minutes before one. We can have our midnight kiss when it turns midnight in California."

Jane looked back and forth like she forgot her lines so Eleanor tries to help get things back on track. "Look, Jane. You and I can deliver her food around four-thirty and still get back to the dance and dinner before anyone notices we're gone. What do you think? Will you help me?" Jane rolls her eyes, catching on. "I guess there is no changing your mind, huh?

Sandy steps closer to the bug, "Thanks Jane, and you're right, there is no changing my mind. I'm going to stay at Jon's place. You and Eleanor are going to slip away with goodies for me and then get back to the party. Fred's in charge of the band at the dance. If you'd like, you can call me and let me hear how things are going. Then, when the fireworks are over, Jon will come back to his place and collect his kiss. Besides it'll be New Year's Eve and I don't think anyone will bother me that night."

With a little whine to her voice, "Okay, I sure hope you're right because you're going to miss the party of the year... This year and next.

Eleanor jumped up. "Oh crap, I smell bread. I hope it's not burning." With that, she was gone to the kitchen. Sandy and Jane follow, telling her they would help. That leaves Jon and Fred with the bug.

"Jon, do you think Sandy will be okay here alone?"

Jon nodded. "I do. The place will be locked up tight and I'll call her all night long, well except from eleven-thirty to when I get back to her. She'll be okay."

Fred moves closer to Jon. "I think you're smart. Most people wouldn't believe a beautiful woman like Sandy would want to be here alone with a crazy man after her, especially on New Year's Eve. Have you checked all the locks and windows in the place?"

Jon answered, "Yep, I even replaced the one at the bottom of the stairs. My side of the alley is secure. How about here in the hotel?"

"Well Jon, all is secure here. The new cameras are in place. That front door is a fortress and difficult to break into. The one back in the alley... Well, I guess you could bust it open. As it is, you can't see the door from the street and I need to install a light out there. I will put that on my list for next week. Most people forget it's there. I'll push the dumpster in front of it to camouflage it during the party."

Jon scratches his head. "So you're telling me that's a vulnerable spot?"

"Yeah, Jon, but you would have to know it is there, then know how to get to the roof of the hotel, then know about the turn mechanism that makes it run, then cross quietly and then get into your side. That's a lot of knowledge that few know and surely not these bad guys. Not to mention they would have to know she was there alone."

"God, I hope you're right."

ELEVEN

NEW YEAR'S EVE PREPARATIONS ALWAYS seem to be busy, whether you're getting ready to go to a party or hosting one. Sandy found that she had nothing to do. She decided to sit on the front porch, wrapped in a blanket to watch the bustle of the little town. All of her assignments were done and in place. She was a little sad she couldn't go to this fireworks shindig, but she understood why. With her tablet in her lap, partially hidden by the blanket she was wrapped in, she continued to research on what to name the bedroom suite that Eleanor and Fred were using.

Surfing the news for any mention of the trial she would be involved in next week, she settled on a news blurb about a fireworks display in Houston at Tinsley Park. When she clicked on it, she knew for certain what she would call the suite.

Jane bounded up the stairs of the porch and stopped at Sandy's feet. "I'm so busy. I wish I could sit and play on a computer."

"I'm not playing, I'm researching. I'll prove it

to you. But first, will you go find Eleanor and ask her if she could she come out here when she has a minute?"

Jane smiled. "Sure, that's who I need to talk to anyway. Be right back."

Sandy smiled to herself. She had the names for the two rooms behind the kitchen. She couldn't wait to share it with the two women she shared so many of her good memories of this town with so far.

Jane arrived first. She must have run. A few seconds later, Eleanor arrived. "What's all the fuss about? Jane said you needed me right away. Thank goodness I was just finishing up for the day."

Sandy frowned at Jane. "I said to ask her when she had a minute, not to drop everything and rush out here. Grab a blanket from the trunk and sit for a minute, now that you're both here. Please."

A few minutes later, all three were snuggled in a blanket close together, listening to Sandy. "I wanted to share with you the names of the two rooms behind the kitchen. The one to the right, the one I stayed in those first few nights, is going to be the Jane Long Room. She was known as the 'Mother of Texas'."

Jane jumped right out of her chair and almost tumbled to the floor. "You're naming a room after me? Well, someone I share a name with. That is so cool. I can't wait to tell Uncle George."

Sandy laughed at Jane's excitement, "Wait before you get excited! You don't even know who she is yet. Do you want to know?"

"Yes, please. I'm sure she's great."

Sandy began again, "Well, to start, her title as 'Mother of Texas' was awarded for the wrong reason, I think. She got the title because she was thought to be the first English-speaking woman to give birth on the Bolivar Peninsula, just outside of Galveston, way back in 1821. Turns out, she wasn't. But to me, after learning about all of her struggles, she definitely earned the title. She gave birth almost alone. She fought starvation for weeks by hunting, ice-fishing, and gathering oysters, until she couldn't anymore in early 1822. She had tried to stay, even when others left, because she was waiting for her husband's return. Jane found out later that he had been captured by Mexican soldiers, taken to Mexico City and accidentally killed while trying to treat injured soldiers there. This made her a widow and single mother of two, fending for herself in quite a primitive, different time. She was alone but it doesn't mean she didn't have offers. Apparently she was quite a catch as there are many historical hints of famous men who courted her. Sam Houston gave the 'Mother of Texas' title to Margaret Theresa Wright in a speech, supposedly in recognition of her support of Texas troops during the Texas Revolution. This intentional switch of titles from Jane to Margaret is rumored to be his way of getting back at Jane for turning him down."

Eleanor was listening to this story added, "She was an independent woman, much like our

Jane. I bet there's more to read about her in the library."

Jane jumped up again to leave. "I have a little extra time. I'm going to the library right now to look. Oh, wait. It's not open today. Oh poo. I'll have to wait till Monday."

Eleanor laughed. "The internet is not closed today, so you can research a little to pass the time till tonight. But Sandy, you said you named both rooms. What's the second one's name? The one Fred and I are in, right?"

Sandy smiled and noticed that Fred and Jon had stepped out on to the porch without a sound and were listening to the announcement of the names. Sandy looked straight at Eleanor, barely containing her excitement. "You're absolutely correct, and I love this one, too."

Jane interrupts, "Is it the Roosevelt Room after Eleanor Roosevelt? She's famous."

Sandy turned towards Jane. "Good guess, but not correct. Eleanor Roosevelt was not a Texan. This room is for Eleanor Tinsley and she was a famous Texan."

Fred huffs, surprising the girls, "Isn't that a person in the Beatles song? Eleanor Rigsby?"

Jon couldn't hold back his laughter. "Sandy said Eleanor Tinsley, with a 'T,' not Rigsby. You're so funny, ol' man."

Sandy wanted Eleanor to hear her reasons and Eleanor looked so confused. Sandy held her hand up for everyone to hush, "Eleanor Whilden Tinsley was named to the Texas Women's Hall of Fame in 1988. She was the daughter of W. C.

Whilden and Georgiabel Burleson, she was born in Dallas and grew up there.

Eleanor interrupts, "I was born in Dallas, too."

"She came from good stock like you. Tinsley earned a bachelor's degree from Baylor University. Didn't you go to Baylor for a year?"

Eleanor is beaming at this question. "Why yes, I sure did. Mamma got sick and I came home to take care of her. I never was able to go back."

"Well from there she got married, moved to Houston and had three children. Most importantly, she was very active in working to end race-based segregation within public and private schools.

In '69, she was elected to the Houston Independent School Board, and soon after she was their board president. She was defeated when she ran for reelection in '73, mostly because of her stand on integration in the Houston schools. She was elected to Houston city council in '79. She worked on limiting billboards, increasing indoor smoking bans, support for gay rights, and more. In '95, when she was forced to retire because she'd reached the maximum limit on terms."

Jane is ready to burst. "She sounds like you Eleanor always helping with everything she can."

Sandy wasn't finished. "That's not all. In '09, she helped elect the Houston's first openly gay mayor, Annise Parker. Clearly retirement didn't suit her. She kept working with Planned Parenthood, the Baptist General Convention of Texas, and she founded the SPARK Park Program, which has created 200 Houston playgrounds and parks. She was a busy woman. Tinsley also served as president of the Texas Council of Child Welfare Boards. She helped establish payment by the state for foster care children not covered by welfare, and for children in the AFDC program."

Jane couldn't contain herself, "wow, she helped with the AFDC program? That is so cool. I was helped with that. It's the Aid to Families with Dependent Children. George said when mom and dad passed in the car accident, he got help from them. Eleanor, you two are really alike. She helped me and so do you. I have so many women to read about! I better go get started."

Jane's excitement was contagious and everyone was smiling at her. Sandy patted Jane on the shoulder. "Yes, you have a bunch of historical women to use as role models, not to mention some present-day ones, too. I think you'll follow in her footsteps. Your research on her will open the door to what you want to focus on next."

Fred was beaming at all this news. "You picked another good name to honor two good Texas women. I especially approve of Tinsley. I hear there is a park in Houston named for her. Maybe we should visit it on our honeymoon? What do you think?"

That earned him a kiss from Eleanor.

A truck slowed in front of the hotel and Owen rolled down his window. "I wish I had time to sit around on a lovely porch like this. Have you noticed the time? Sandy, you're late. The team is worried. I'm here to see why she hasn't arrived yet. Jane, your uncle told me to bring you home if I could. So, come along, I'm headed there now."

Jane jumped up and hugged Eleanor and Sandy and hurried off to get in Owen's truck. Fred and Eleanor said their goodbyes. Jon helped Sandy with her things so they could head over to the library and deliver her into the safe hands of the agents there.

Jon and Sandy locked up the front of the library as they came in and headed to the fourth floor. All the windows had furniture or boxes blocking any view from the outside. It would spoil the whole plan if the bad guys could see how many were here. They would quickly realize it was a set up. Sandy sat down on the loveseat and the team captain of this group, Mitch, turned to Sandy.

"We were getting a little worried. Glad you're here. Before Jon leaves, we want to go over the plans one more time." Sandy was happy to listen to this again. Jon settled in beside her on the loveseat.

"Ok, then. Agent MacNamara, you met her when her team set this place up, is in the mobile unit out at the auction house. Her team will monitor all our cameras and listening devices from there. The eight of us here are armed and ready for a small invasion, plus others are watching for movement around town. There have been whispers from our informants that Pete took the bait and will be here sometime tonight. We think between six-thirty and ten p.m. Most of the activities at the auction house will be in full tilt by then."

Sandy asked, "I count ten of you. Who are the extras?"

Mitch moved close to two men who were similar in size and shape and coloring of Owen and Jon. "This is John and Gary. They will leave to get food and then return around seven. They will go out to the auction house to get food, and swap coats and the like with Owen and Jon. They'll return here with food enough for just three. The two of them and you. That way, Owen and Jon will appear to be at the auction house, but be able to be here. The bad guys will see them coming and going, but not get good looks at the faces due to the clothing and scarves on these guys.

Sandys spirits soar. She had no idea that Jon would be here. That was the best news ever. "I'm so glad that Jon will be here, Oh and Owen, too. Why go to such lengths?"

Mitch walked back to the other group. "This team is a highly trained SWAT team and has been arriving slowly during library hours for the last two days. They are here to capture, or kill if necessary, whoever comes for you. If Pete comes himself then he has sealed his fate without the need for a lengthy trial."

"Okay, I understand their presence, but Owen and Jon?" Sandy was missing something.

"Owen and Jon are here because they asked. We're going to the trouble of them being seen at the Auction House because we think that there will be someone there watching. I'm sure Pete and his gang believe that you will have someone here with you and we want them to think it's just John, Gary, and me. After the swap, it will be Owen, Jon and me. Gary and John will stay at the party and watch who leaves, then follow or detain them. Besides, Owen and Jon know everyone in these parts and can identify any townie that chooses not to go out to the auction house."

Sandy was nervous about tonight but knowing that Jon and Owen would be here had settled her immensely. "Well… Let's get this show on the road."

"My thoughts exactly." Jon was up and moving. He planted a kiss on Sandy and headed out. Time was going to tick off slowly until he returned.

Sandy stood and grabbed her bag. "I think I'm going to go sit at the kitchen table in the apartment and try to do some research."

Mitch advanced with Gary to the door as if there might be a wild animal behind the closed door, tucking Sandy behind him. Sandy waited as directed and minutes later she heard the all-clear signal. She knew they needed to be careful, and appreciated that, but it still unnerved her.

Mitch met her at the door. "Do you mind keeping the door open? And if one of us asks you if everything is ok and you answer 'it's okay' or 'I'm fine,' we'll know there's a problem, so be creative in your answers like, "its perfect' or 'all is well,' ok?" Oh, and for tonight, can you wear this?"

Mitch had a woman's bulletproof vest in his hand. Sandy took it and then looked back at Mitch. "You think this is necessary?"

He pulled back his shirt to show that he was wearing and, at that, Sandy added the vest to her clothing.

With her sweatshirt over the vest, Sandy left the door open and was grateful for the verbal safety code. She sat down at the table to work. Women in Texas had been so much fun to research and later use in her décor. Not being from here, it was so interesting and gave her so many ideas for travel. Tinsley Park was definitely on the list.

She needed to have something to focus on, so the plans for the third floor would have to do. She planned to take the six small rooms and reconfigure them into three large spaces. Two of the rooms would have a door between them, making them adjoining so a large family could reserve them together. Taking out a couple of walls and adding a bathroom would be the big work on that floor. The hardwood floors just need a little TLC and finishing. So, a theme is what she needed for décor. For sure one would be dedicated to Caro Crawford Brown.

Sandy had read about this fearless journalist, Caro Crawford Brown. She could really relate to this woman. Sandy also admired anyone who won a Pulitzer, but to win because of your work on a dangerous case like hers, well that made her worth honoring. She won her Pulitzer Prize for local journalism in 1955. Her work helped dismantle the power of infamous political boss George Parr. Brown worked for the Alice Daily Echo and she was assigned to cover Parr after a previous reporter was killed while investigating the Parr family. Sandy was so impressed with her bravery that she chose her pen name, C.C. Brown, as a reminder of Caro's willingness to do what was right. An example of her unwavering integrity, Brown was warned by the Texas Rangers that her life was in danger for her work covering George Parr, and so she always carried a pistol in her glove compartment for protection. Despite the fact that she was working to take him down, Brown had scrupulous ethics, and at one point even saved Parr's life by physically inserting herself between Parr and a Texas Ranger when he was about to shoot Parr.

For the next twenty minutes, Sandy spent her time saving information and pictures to be used as part of her brochure that she would have in each room for the guests to read. Sandy had come to love this part as much as pulling all the color and décor together. It made her feel like a small part of history, ensuring that these women were not forgotten.

Part of the antiques she had acquired from the auction barn was a lovely selection of furniture from the fifties. Her plans were for the room to be a throwback to that era, an elegant portrait of a time gone by.

One namesake down and two to go for the

third floor. The next room would be the Johnson Room, but not for LBJ or Lady Bird, even though they were very fine Texans. It would be named for Lizzie Johnson. Her family moved to Texas when she was four. Even though her first career was as a school teacher, she later became a cattle baroness, just as successful as other famous names of that time. In 1871, she registered her own cattle brand and purchased 10 acres of land to start her own cattle business. She became known as one of the early Texas Cattle Queens, and was the first woman to ride on the famed Chisholm Trail with her livestock.

This woman had it all. She was smart, a good communicator, and knew a good investment when she saw it. Sandy wanted that, too. She spent another few minutes saving and creating her pages for the binder for that room, too.

Mitch softly knocked on the door and came into the kitchen. "You okay? You've been so quiet. Thought I'd tell you that Gary and John left, and Owen and your Jon should be here in the next thirty minutes."

Sandy didn't try to hide her screen, she kind of wanted someone's opinion of these two women and maybe she could run the third one by him. "Mitch, would you like to see my ideas? I'm naming all the rooms at the B&B after famous Texas women."

Mitch moved closer and looked over her shoulder at her work. "Dang, that's impressive. I like both. Who's number three?"

Sandy changed screens and said, "This third

room is the Parker room, for Cynthia Ann Parker. Her father established Fort Parker and was said to negotiate with the Indians around him in a peaceful, non-intrusive way. Not understanding that all the Indians he made treaties with were not of the same tribe, his people were attacked and most killed. Some escaped and some were taken as prisoners. Cynthia was eight or nine when this happened. She spent twenty-four years with her new family. She was adopted, given a new name, married and had three children with the Comanche leader Peta Nacona."

Mitch leaned back in the chair beside Sandy. "Wow, that is a story that should be a movie. I am sure that story scared the pants off the settlers."

Sandy smiled. "Yes, I am sure early settler moms worried about just that and Cynthia was returned to her white family and her story captured the hearts of Texans and well, the whole country. She was even given land and a pension from the government. I even thought about naming the room Naduah which means someone found. It was her Indian name. I know I will mention both names in her brochure."

Mitch seemed to be in his own world. "So how did she get back home? And what happened next?"

Sandy took a deep breath and finished the story for him. "The infamous Texas Ranger, Lawrence Sullivan Ross led a raid near the Pease River and she and her infant daughter were captured. That happened in 1860, in 1864 the daughter died of pneumonia and Cynthia wanted to return to her sons but her brother would not allow it. Grief stricken and many failed attempts of escape, she refused to eat or drink. She died at the age of forty-five in 1871."

Mitch stood to return to the office area. He stopped and turned. "That, like your other stories, is an amazing look into our Texas history. Women came a long way and shaped our state. It's about time we value not just women but all those who shaped our Texas."

Mitch sat back down beside Sandy. "Staying at your B&B is on my to-do list when this is over and you have it open." Before Sandy could answer, the large window by the bed crashed and Mitch turned the table over and pulled Sandy behind it. "Stay down and move only if I say so."

Owen and Jon parked in the alley so that they could check on the back door of Sandy's B&B. The dumpster had been moved and just as they headed for the library entrance, knowing that the bad guys were here, a loud explosion of glass could be heard raining down from above. Jon knew it had to be his window because it was raining down on them from his side of the alley. That was right where Sandy should be. Owen took shelter from the falling glass, then was up the fire escape on the library side without a word. Gunshots were heard from inside and out. Even from where Jon had sheltered from the falling glass, he could see that the ladder from the B&B was extended to the library, which meant the bad guys were on his side of the alley, too. Jon took cover just long enough to send out the mayday text. Help would be on the way.

As soon as he pushed send, he started to the front of the library knowing he could go up the stairs to the fourth floor without having to stop on each floor. It was a straight shot. Once he got to the front door, Jon had to fish out his new keys because surprisingly, it was still locked. He let the alarm to go off so that everyone nearby would know bad things were happening.

The door to the fourth floor takes another precious moment to unlock. Jon has his gun out and ready to shoot if anything moved around him. He moved up the stairs towards the fourth floor as quickly as he could.

TWELVE

SANDY COULD HEAR SHOUTS AND gunfire from the office area and outside. It sounded like a war. It felt like it was from everywhere. Sandy looked toward the door to the bathroom and stairs that went down to the front of the building. Could she get that far? Mitch was already thinking of that and was pulling the heavy, stainless-steel kitchen table to the door. With the movement of the table, bullets started pinging off of it and hitting the walls around them. Another window crashed behind them. Hopefully, the stray shots were the cause of it shattering and not someone coming in from that window.

Sandy heard Owen shout from what sounded like the roof. Everything goes dead quiet for a minute. Mitch takes this moment to peer around the table while still inching back toward the door and the stairs. Sandy's head is spinning, but she made herself focus on the here and now. As they got to the door, Mitch chances a look again and takes a bullet to the shoulder. It was a graze, but it started bleeding immediately. "Get out that door and down the stairs. People should be on the way since Owen is here." Sandy hesitated but Mitch says, "Go," and so she did.

Owen entered the fourth floor through the window closest to the office and took out, what he hoped, was the last of the bad guys. He had already eliminated two on the roof who were by the rope that was used to break the big window in the apartment, where someone had entered.

As the last man hit the floor, one of the SWAT team members that had been pinned down was at the apartment door, and another group was by the bathroom door that leads into the Jack and Jill bathroom for the apartment. Hand gestures instead of voice command had the eight-man team dividing into four teams.

Two left by the main stairs, two to the roof, two to the bathroom, and two to the apartment door. Owen followed the team to the apartment.

Jon could hear commotion above him on the fourth floor and also in this stairwell but he was careful not to add any noise to it. He wanted his entrance to be a surprise. He was inching his way up. He wanted to run, but these old stairs creaked and groaned enough without his weight running up them.

Sandy got to the door and stepped inside to the dark. Lights were her last thought. Using the wall for guidance, she inched her way to the bathroom door, where the stairs were just beyond it. The bathroom was dark and quiet. She passed it and reached the new door to the stairs and unlocked it. As she opened the door, noise came from everywhere; the apartment, the bathroom, everything seemed to shake... Or was it her? Her inner voice was saying, hurry, open the door and run as fast as you can down and outside. That last second, before her legs listened and started running, she felt hands grab her and pull her in tight. He was so close. Pete's voice came into her ear from behind her. He had been in the bathroom, waiting. He hisses, "You're mine. Don't worry, baby. Don't I always take care of you?"

Sandy could feel that he was sexually excited. This is what turned him on? Just one more reason to get away from him. His husky voice continued, "I'll take care of you in more ways than one. The first way will be for me, and the second will be to fix your big mouth."

Pete was groping around her body, trying to pull her sweat pants down when it finally clicked and Sandy realized what he had planned for her. Rape her and then kill her. All those brave Texas women ran through her mind and time stood still. They wouldn't give up or give in.

Fight or flight? Fight, Sandy tells herself. She was going to fight. She drops to her knees letting all her weight bring him over her. She was hoping to push him down the stairs when he was off balance. Maybe the fall would kill him, but for sure she could run the other way back to Mitch and his gun if it worked.

It worked! When she went limp and bent over, he released her just enough for her to back up and turn. She ran right into a wall of human male flesh. He held her tight, turned and passed her on to someone else, then he disappeared through the door and down the stairs after Pete.

Sandy was pulled back into the apartment and in the light where she could see that this man was one of the SWAT members, and Owen was there, too.

The word "crossfire" and then two shots ring out and more bodies disappeared through the door. Sandy bounded for the light switch for the stairs. Who else could be in the stairwell?

One eternally long minute later, a string of men and Jon with a bloody Pete in cuffs come out of the stairwell. Jon was bleeding from the nose and on his left arm, but other than that he seemed okay.

Pete was alive, cursing, and struggling against the cuffs but he couldn't escape the big hands that were holding him. One of the men who had Pete spoke softly, "Stop resisting. It's over." Pete stopped dead when he saw Sandy. "You bitch. All you're good for is fucking. Don't think this is over. Your precious dad and Uncle Bob are getting their turn right now. There will be more surprises to come, just you wait and see." Pete was hauled away into the fourth-floor office area, shouting all kinds of threats of things to come.

Owen was on his phone. "You're about to be attacked. Take cover."

Mitch jumped on his phone, too. "Bring the mobile unit to the library, we need to process this place. All assets are alive and well. We think Sandy's dad and Bob Manley are in imminent danger. Alert the teams there." Both conversations were crazy.

Owen and Jon set up the kitchen table and chairs, and put Sandy in one. Owen starts, "Your dad knows what to do and he's not alone either. Not since Bob was tracked and attacked. Jaime is there, too. We will get a report soon."

Jon had Sandy by the hands and he slightly shivers as one of the guys was applying a bandage to his left arm above the elbow, Jon looked at the officer dressing his wound. "Report."

"Sir, it's just a graze wound. The doc is on his way. Two of our team members need a hospital and he's seeing to them first. There are two nurses here, too. They have a member of our team with some injuries from the glass. Aside from Pete, only three others of his group survived. In total, there are nine fatalities. Eight are from here, all perps. The other attempted to follow you two from the party and got into a gunfight with Gary and John, who were following him, sir."

Jon nodded. "Thank you."

Sandy was stunned. Pete brought twelve men with him, just for her? How many had he sent after Dad, Bob, and Jaime? She hoped they were okay.

Once Jon's arm was bandaged, he and Owen decided to cover the big window. Fred had arrived with a roll of black plastic to tape over it until the window guy could come by and fix it. "Not going to happen on the first, that being a holiday, so we'll have to wait till the second to start that project," Fred said as he checked Sandy over. "I promised Jane and Eleanor I would personally verify you were fine. They're still at the party. It was all I could do to keep them there when the alarm went out. The fireworks don't start for an hour, so please think about coming over to the auction house to close out this year and bring in the next."

Sandy hadn't even thought about that. "Is everyone okay out there?"

Fred nodded. "Right as rain. Mostly relieved everyone is okay here. Even the two going to the hospital will be good as new with a little time off. So, we have lots to celebrate."

Owen, Fred, and Jon almost had the plastic taped and two sheets of plywood in place on the two windows when Owen's phone went off. "Hello? Yes... Okay... Yes, she's right here... Sure." Owen handed the phone to Sandy and Jon stepped behind her, hoping that the news was good, but if not, he was there to catch her.

"Daddy? Oh, daddy you're okay? Yes, I'm fine thanks to this bunch of brave men. How about Bob and Jaime?" Jon could feel her relax and even feel her smile without even seeing her face. Jon was sure there was a story there, too.

Sandy says her goodbyes and giggled. "Dad is coming here in two days. He has to be in Dallas for the trial on the seventh, so we'll go from here together. He should get here on the third. I can't wait to hug him!"

Fred clapped his hands. "I guess we need to put a few finishing touches on those rooms on the second floor, so your dad and company will have a place to stay near you. Eleanor and I will talk about it tonight. I'm heading back now so I can deliver news in person. Hey, wait. Can you take a selfie so I can send it now?"

Jon took the phone, snapped the picture and sent it before anyone could say a word. Sandy was glad she had managed a smile.

With that, Jon turned to everyone,."This girl needs a few quiet moments. She's had a crazy New Year's Eve. If she feels like it, and if the team thinks all is safe, we can make the fireworks."

Jon looked into Sandy's eyes and then kissed her. "This building is a crime scene. Your place was used to make entry, but we think they just ran through it. Let's go to your fourth floor and regroup. I hear you have a lovely shower area and comfy loveseat. And Eleanor has leftover meatloaf in the kitchen for you. What do you think?"

There were no words needed. Sandy grabbed him by the hand and handed Owen the rest of the tape for the window and headed out of this crime scene. "Come on, Mr. Retired Texas Ranger. Maybe we can get into a little mischief over there. You know, I wasn't hungry until you mentioned Eleanor's famous meatloaf, so let's go."

With that nightmarish event over, Sandy took a minute to look at the clock in the lobby of the B&B. It was just ten p.m. "You get the meatloaf. I'm going for a shower, clean clothes and then some alone time with you."

Sandy bounded up the stairs to the fourth floor. She didn't worry about making noise or even bother with checking around corners. If she had, she might have seen the man waiting with the gun.

"Stop right there! Where's Pete? He told me to wait here for him." This small man was pointing a gun at her, but not with much intent of harm. Sandy had startled him and herself.

"Uhhh… Pete's still in the other building. He'll be here soon. He let me come over here to get ready." Sandy was trying to dial her phone without this man noticing. She hoped Jon would pick up and listen.

"Who are you? Pete didn't say anyone was over here."

Sandy introduced herself, hoping that Pete had planned to keep her alive and had spread that intention around his goons.

This man still looked nervous. His hand was shaking. He tried to steady himself by holding the gun with both hands. He spoke in a voice that said he was trying to decide if he should trust Sandy or not. "He must have convinced you to marry him seeing as how he let you come alone. He's not an easy man to persuade. He must really trust and love you."

Sandy had her face schooled so this man wouldn't get suspicious. Sandy smiled and tried to look shy. "He should be right behind me. Can you put the gun down? You're making me nervous with that thing. I need to pack quickly. What's your name?"

He slowly lowered the gun. "I'm Reverend Black. I'm here to perform your wedding ceremony."

Sandy nearly choked, but hid it with a cough. "That's so sweet of you to come all this way on New Year's Eve to make this a momentous day. I have to shower and change. There's a love seat inside here. Come on in and rest for a minute while I get ready."

Sandy and Reverend Black stepped inside her space and he sat unsuspectingly on the loveseat. He was an older, stout and short man in a black suit that didn't fit him very well. He looked like he'd slept in his clothes. He didn't seem to notice Sandy had a phone in her hand. He put the gun on the cushion of the sofa. The loveseat had its back to the door, so when he sat down his view of the room kept him from seeing the open door. Sandy had left the door open on purpose, for Jon.

Sandy backed into the bathroom but before she could close the door, her phone buzzed. It startled her so badly that she almost lost it in the toilet. When she got control, she opened it up to look at the screen. Maybe the call didn't go through and she was on her own. Reverend Brown asked, "Is that Pete?"

Sandy looked up wide-eyed, and replied as calmly as she could. "Why yes, it is Pete. He just texted and wanted to know if you're still here. I am going to tell him yes, and to hurry it up."

Reverend Black nodded and smiled. "That's wonderful. You hurry along. Don't want to be late for your own wedding."

Sandy closed the bathroom door and texted back to Jon, "Help. Locked myself in bathroom. Armed man with back to door. Be careful."

Jon had read the text and, after seeing what Sandy was dealing with, got help and started up with his handgun ready. He stopped outside the door to text her back just as reinforcements arrived. After a few minutes, Sandy could hear several male voices shouting orders to the Reverend.

Jon finally came to the bathroom door and said, "He's gone and we are sweeping the whole place, even the basement... No more surprises. I have a guard posted at the door. Take your shower. I will be right back." Sandy didn't even answer. He was out the door and gone before her brain could connect with her mouth. The reinforcements were meticulously checking every nook and cranny. That lapse in due diligence could have been a deadly mistake.

The meatloaf that had been heating up in the oven for their dinner was ruined. Jon hoped that maybe Sandy would be up to going to the fireworks show to snuggle up and relax amidst her new family and friends, who were just as happy as he was that she was here in Twin Creeks.

THIRTEEN

IN JON'S TRUCK AND ALMOST to the auction house, Sandy put her hand on his. "Thanks for being there for me tonight. I'm glad we are going to bring in the new year together. It's wonderful to know that I can do this forever with you."

Jon turned to look at Sandy but barely dodges an armadillo crossing the road in front of them. Both laugh. Jon had that goofy smile on his face that's so charming and made Sandy want to climb into his lap and kiss him.

Sandy and Jon decided to set up the lawn chairs in the bed of his truck, which felt like such a Texan thing to do. Music began to play and everyone started to sing along. "The stars at night, are big and bright, deep in the heart of Texas." Everyone knows the words and just as the song ended, the fireworks explode. The show lasts about twenty minutes. Sparklers are handed out and it's so lovely to see the townsfolk here having this moment together. Afterwards, everyone heads back to their vehicles to go back into town.

Jon and Sandy make it back just before one.

Sandy had turned to look out the back window of the truck as they were on the rise just before the city limits. She could see lots of cars in the distance behind them. They had all made it back to town together. It could have passed as a nighttime parade. This cold, crisp night was lit up by the parade of headlights. Jon parked his truck out in front of the B&B and climbed to the porch with Sandy tucked at his side. "This has been one long day." Sandy was fishing around in her purse when Jon said, "I have the keys you gave me, no worries."

"Oh, I know. I was looking for my car keys. I parked it down the street in the closed hardware store parking lot. The workers were parked in front of the B&B. I haven't moved it in three days and I can't remember if I locked it."

Jon scrunched his nose. "Will it even work from here?"

Sandy pulled her keys out, "It has before." She then pointed her key fob and pressed the button, expecting to hear a sweet little chirp as usual. Instead, there was a boom. Both Jon and Sandy hit the porch, hoping the blast wouldn't send flying objects their way.

People came from everywhere. Some were still in their cars, coming back from the fireworks display. The fire station a block away lit up, too and the doors started to open. Something big hit the balcony above them and Sandy's car was ablaze. The blast also dropped the wall to the hardware store and shouts rang out about the balcony above them being on fire.

Safety requirements called for fire extinguishers on every floor. Jon grabbed one as he headed up the stairs to the second floor. The Eberly Rooms balcony was on fire. Well, the cushions on the chairs were. Jon quickly put the blazes out and noticed that the honeymoon suite had smoke wafting out from under the door. Sandy had followed him up with another extinguisher and was on her way to check the other floors.

Jon yelled, "Sandy, be careful opening doors. I'll be right up, as soon as I take care of the honeymoon suite."

In the honeymoon suite, a metal piece that broke through the window had landed in the middle of the bed linens and they were smoldering, but thankfully not ablaze. It was an easy fix.

Sandy made it to the third floor and found nothing amiss and her fourth floor was okay, too. What a relief! From her window seat, she could see the firemen had arrived and had started to put out the fire caused by the explosion. Her car, of course, would be a total loss. Jon walked up behind her and leaned in, "I guess that was Pete's New Year's surprise he was ranting about. What a maniac." There were no more words to say. Both just stood and watched.

A few minutes later, Owen and Dylan came rushing in with guns drawn in one hand and a fire extinguisher in the other. Jon glanced over and said, "Everything in here seems okay but Sandy's car is gone. A few cushions on the second-floor balcony, a window and some linens in the honeymoon suite. I guess the worst is our nerves. Sandy is still shaking."

Owen advanced toward them after he holstered his gun. "Jon, where's this blood from?"

Jon turned to find Dylan and Owen staring at his face where there was blood trickling down his cheek. Jon reached up to touch it when Sandy grabbed his hand. "Jon, there's a piece of glass embedded along your jaw, just below your ear. It needs to be removed."

Jon hadn't even felt it. He was too busy putting out fires, literally. Dylan was on the phone and directing a paramedic up to them after describing the wound.

Owen pulled out a chair for Jon to sit on and then turned to Sandy. "Come here, let's see if you're leaking anywhere like Jon." She wasn't, thank God.

The paramedic arrived and started on Jon. Owen reported that Sandy looked okay.

Jon's jaw needed three stitches in an awkward place. The paramedic warned Jon against talking too much, and that he should chew slowly and gently to avoid the wound from reopening. Jon was also advised to get a tetanus shot.

Owen hung up his phone. "There's a bomb squad on its way from Abilene to check over the whole place. Martha wants you over at the café to wait till they're done. I already sent Fred and Eleanor there."

Sandy's head jerked up with a look of surprise. "So, you think he rigged more booby traps inside the B&B? Are Eleanor and Fred okay?"

Jon stood and took Sandy's hand. "We left

before Eleanor and Fred so they probably saw the explosion coming back. Come on, let's get out of here and let them work. Since Pete and company had time to plant one in your car, they might have in here, too. We left here early yesterday, and so did all the workers, giving them plenty of time to do most anything. And earlier, when they checked the place over, they weren't looking for bombs. They were looking for bad guys."

Sandy had thought that when they caught Pete, it was over, but that didn't seem to be the case. Pete had shouted at her that it was not over and she would pay, but it hadn't occurred to her that it was anything more than angry words and empty threats. She zipped up her jacket and left with Jon, nodding to Owen and Dylan. The commotion outside was jarring. There were so many people boarding up windows that were broken from the explosion, news reporters, the looky-loos, and of course, the fire department. Martha's café was a bright beacon across the courthouse lawn. She welcomed Sandy and Jon with a choice of hot chocolate, coffee, or something stronger.

Eleanor waved them over to the comfy booth in the back. "We got the hot chocolate. I wanted something stronger for my nerves but Fred said we needed to keep our wits about us."

Sandy agreed and requested the hot chocolate, too. "Are you two going to go to your home out on the other side of town? I would, if I were you."

Fred spoke, "We've been talking about it, but we wanted to see you and Jon before we left. You are welcome to come with us. I know its a thirty-minute drive, but there's a bed to sleep in and shower."

Jon answered for Sandy, "That's a tempting offer but with both buildings open and so many folks out and about, we might be needed. Tomorrow for us will definitely be a stay in bed kind of day."

"Don't you mean today? It is almost two in the morning. Happy New Year to us," Eleanor drawled.

Sandy groaned, "Please don't remind me. This booth looks better and better by the second." Before anyone could answer, Mike popped into the café with good news. "Hey, Sandy and Jon. I just got word that your fourth floor at the library is clear. The crime scene crew is moving over to your car and the B&B. So, if you want to go there, you can. It's messy but safe."

Sandy was up and moving. She returned her cup and Jon's to the counter and was leaving the café. Jon hurried to follow and Eleanor got up too, with Fred following. At the door to the café, several of the firemen came in looking for food and drink after battling the explosion and fire. Sandy stopped, "thank you for taking care of what's left of my car."

"No worries ma'am. It's our job. Sorry about your Jeep." Martha was already directing them to a table. She had a tray of ice water with her.

Jon held the door for everyone. "Thank you again. Night, all."

The trip to the fourth floor didn't take long,

and Sandy and Jon curled up next to each other not only for warmth but for the safe feeling of being alive and together. The apartment was cooler than normal due to the two windows being tapped and covered with plywood, but all was dry and quiet.

Sleep came easy. Exhaustion does that.

FOURTEEN

SANDY WOKE TO THE SMELL of bacon and biscuits. Jon must be in the kitchen fixing his famous biscuits, bacon, and gravy. She started to head for the kitchen just as she was when she heard another male voice. Yikes! She backed up to grab a robe. It's probably better to have clothes on. That was when she recognized the voices. One was her dad. She needed more than a robe; she needed clothes.

When Sandy entered the kitchen, her dad and Uncle Bob were sitting at the kitchen table. When they'd heard about the Jeep explosion, they had jumped in dad's suburban and drove all night.

"Dad, Uncle Bob, I'm so glad to see you."

Sandy's dad stood and tucked Sandy into a long hug. "We stopped in at the café. It's a happening kind of place. We couldn't figure out where you were, but everyone at the café knew, and I mean everyone. I guess you're the talk of the town."

Uncle Bob got his hug next. "Yep, I think the whole town is there and wants all of us there to celebrate once they figured out who you are to us. Even met the car dealership owner. Your dad ordered you a new Jeep from him. Made his day."

Jon pointed at the place setting. "You need to eat. Your dad has orders from Martha to either bring the two of us to the café so people can see we are okay, or the whole bunch is coming here. Thank goodness he chose to come get us, but they won't wait forever."

Sandy sat and enjoyed the food, but mostly the company. "Okay, men. Let's make a stop at the café and then the B&B so dad and Uncle Bob can get settled in."

Dad put his hand on Sandy's. "I know you're not a little girl and the last week or so has been crazy for all of us, but this man has asked me for your hand in marriage. Since you're not handcuffed or anything of the sort, I guess he's the one. Should I say yes? Bob and I are old, but I think we could take him if need be so you could escape. Just say the word."

For a quick moment, Sandy started to panic but Jon's smile made her lean over and kiss her dad on the cheek. "Yes, Dad. Say Yes."

Sandy had worried about how to tell her Dad and Uncle Bob about Jon, but she could see that that struggle was avoided by Jon meeting them alone and fixing them breakfast.

Bob was impressed that Jon had been a ranger and clearly felt Sandy was in excellent hands.

Uncle Bob was right, Martha's place was packed. Martha met us at the door. "Well it's about time. I hadn't planned on being open today, but with everyone knocking on the door, I had to. Best spontaneous New Year's Day party ever, thanks to you."

Sandy looked around and it was like a party. The flat screens had parades on with talk of football games to be next. People were making dad and Uncle Bob feel welcome. Rick Waller came over and asked Sandy what color she wanted the Jeep to be. After an hour or so, they all headed to the B&B to see how much damage had been done. On the way there, they detoured to inspect the carcass of Sandy's bombed car.

When they turned toward the B&B, they could see Fred and Eleanor out on the front porch sitting in the rocking chairs, waiting for them to arrive.

Fred was up and shaking hands. "Hi there, I'm Fred and this here is my fiancée, Eleanor. I'm the general contractor working for Miss McAllister, helping her to get this place back into working order. I figure there's a new list to tend to after last night's fire."

Jon stepped up and unlocked the front door. "Don't let Fred fool you, he and Eleanor are more than the contractors. They're dear friends."

Sandy was surprised that the lobby area was in such good shape after having an army of people through it just a few hours ago. The surprise was all over Sandy's face. When she looked at Eleanor, she winked and Sandy knew that the two of them had already been here and worked on things.

This was just another reason why she knew Twin Creeks was her place in the world.

Sandy started for the stairs. "Come on dad, Uncle Bob. Let me show you the finished rooms that you'll be staying in. One has a broken window, but we should have it fixed up no time."

Sandy could see Eleanor had been in there, too. There was plywood on the window in the Eberly Room, which Bob had picked to be his room. That put dad in the Dickerson Room.

Dad picked up the binder in his room. "I love this idea. Tonight, I'll read all about my room's namesake. Are you doing this for each room?"

Sandy was beaming. "I'm glad you like my idea. As we go to the next floor, which is not done yet, I'll tell you those names, too. My place is on the fourth floor."

Bob chimed in, "I want to see the ladder thing on the roof! It sounds amazing."

Sandy's expression said it all. "I'll let Jon show you that. It's not my favorite place. Besides, it's cold out there. I'm going back to the lobby. I'll meet you boys down there."

The men went up to the roof and Sandy and Eleanor went the lobby. Sandy grabbed her tablet on the way out of her space. She wanted to show Dad and Bob what else she had researched.

Sandy and Eleanor were in the kitchen when the four arrived. Owen came in with them. He had come in from the front door as they came down the stairs.

Owen greeted Sandy and Eleanor. "Good morning ladies. As I was telling the guys, I'm glad we did a thorough check of the place. We found two more gifts from Pete. Neither were as dangerous as the car, but deadly enough."

Eleanor gasped and Sandy stopped dead and steeled herself. "Go on. Tell us."

Bob, dad, Fred, and Jon took seats at the big kitchen table. Owen started in, "Okay, there was a gas canister in the furnace that would have affected the first floor mostly since the others have individual heating/cooling systems. When it heated up, it would have emitted toxic gas into the vents on the first floor. It probably wouldn't have killed anyone, but it would have made people pretty sick for a week or so. On the roof, there was a tripwire at the door that would have released the chimney pipe causing it to fall on whoever tripped it, creating serious bodily harm. All is fixed and the place is safe."

For the next five minutes, the men asked and answered questions thrown out for discussion. Sandy sat perfectly still. Her head was spinning again. When would this end? Was it over? No, there was still the trial.

As the questions were asked and answered, Owen zipped his jacket up. "Happy New Year, folks. I'm heading out to watch the games with my brothers. Liam said he didn't remember what I looked like since I've been wrapped up with this case. Better keep the tribe happy by showing up for their pow wows." Jon walked Owen to the door and a few minutes later returned to hear Sandy telling Bob about the B&B names.

Uncle Bob noticed Sandy's disconnect from the questions and answers, so he decided to try to bring Sandy out of her daydreaming nightmare.

"Tell me about the first floor. You said there is a story here, too.

Sandy smiled at his interest. Bob was a native Texan, but she wasn't sure how much he knew about the women in Texas. "Okay, Bob, here goes. The two rooms on the first-floor that face each other as you step in the front door are the library and dining room. Since long before Texas' advancement to statehood in 1845, Texas has yielded some incredible women. There are artists and musicians, writers, ranchers, politicians, mathematicians, and scientists who have helped shape Texas into what it is today. Two of them were Clara Driscoll and Adina de Zavala. These two women faced off against and with each other to save the Alamo compound. By the late 1880s, the Alamo compound had had many owners, and had fallen into disrepair before it was finally designated as a historical monument. Thanks to the Daughters of the Republic of Texas, Adina, and Clara, the Alamo and the amazing history it preserves was saved. Without these two women, many of Texas' historical sites would have been swallowed up in the name of progress."

Sandy had started out just talking to Bob, but somewhere in her story the rest had quieted and were listening, too. Sandy's dad stirred the pot, so to speak, knowing his words would get a rise out of his daughter.

"So, the men were out fighting and the women were home, saving the state."

Sandy lowered her chin, looked straight at him with a sly smile. "Dad, you should be careful. I'm learning a lot from these brave, Texas women. So, mind your P's and Q's. These two protectors of Texas history worked hard, sometimes together and sometimes against each other, in order to protect and preserve crucial Texas historical sites and artifacts. Adina was a writer and was the granddaughter of Lorenzo de Zavala, the first vice-president of the Republic of Texas. Clara was a strong businesswoman who founded Austin's newspaper, the American-Statesman, among many other business ventures. No weak women here."

Eleanor had been listening closely like she always did when Sandy was telling her stories. "What did you mean when you said they fought each other? I mean, the Alamo is the Alamo."

Sandy smiled at Eleanor. "Well, an argument erupted between the two over the fate of the long barracks, part of the Alamo. Clara offered to tear down the dilapidated building as part of the Daughters of the Republic of Texas' reconstruction efforts, but Adina argued that it was an original part of the building and a vital part of Alamo history. The governor at that time sided with Adina and asked for it to be restored. The case went to court, and the nicely-preserved property full of history we have today is due to that court battle."

Eleanor was clapping. "I can't wait to tell Jane about the two strong women holding up the first floor of this building. Have you figured out who the girl in the photos is yet? I know you've been working on that, too."

Sandy's secret is out. Sandy's dad asks, "Who is she talking about? Have I seen these photos? I'd like to help in that research."

Sandy had been saving her unknown girl for last. "I found old photos of this girl that must have lived here, or at the very least worked here. I wanted to dedicate the lobby to her. I just haven't figured out her name and what she did here. Everyone is welcome to help. She's been a project since day one, when I found the box of old photos and papers." Sandy thought this puzzle would be hers alone to solve, but here she was with five people staring at her, waiting.

Sandy relaxed her shoulders. "I guess my unknown lady becomes a group project starting today. I don't know much. I have photos, letters and some clothing in a suitcase. I'll go get them and we can look them over together." With that announcement, Sandy is up and on her way to the fourth floor to retrieve the box.

Eleanor was up giving everyone paper and pencil for notes. "I'm excited to be a part of this. Take notes about what you observe in the photos and letters, then we can share them."

Fred was also up and moving, but he was heading out of the kitchen. "I'll help, but I have the last piece of a wall on the third floor that needs to be cleared away before the workers come to finish the new wall tomorrow. It should take thirty minutes or so. Be right back."

Bob started to follow. "I can help if you need it."

Fred answered, "Nah, it's a tight fit and

something is keeping it in place. I will have to swing a hatchet to get through. The rest of the wall just fell away but this small place is being difficult."

Jon, Sandy's dad and Bill cleared the table. Sandy returned and pulled out her treasures from the old wooden box. When Uncle Bob is handed the box to set it out of the way. "Hey, this box is probably worth a small fortune all by itself." Sandy, Bill and Eleanor just stare, but Jon picks it up, takes a good look at it and nods. "Bob, I think you could be right. This looks like it held bottles of beer from the Pearl Brewery in San Antonio. That brewery was established back in the 1880's, if I remember correctly. The Pearl Brewery was, at one time, the largest brewery in Texas. That was mainly thanks to Emma Koehler. This looks like it's as old as the brewery."

Bill took the box from Jon and looked it over, too. Sandy didn't care so much about the box, even though she thought it would look good on a shelf displayed in her lobby, but when he mentioned the name Emma, she started digging in her pile. "Look! These letters are addressed to 'Em'. Did she come from these parts? Was she originally from San Antonio?"

Jon shook his head. "I took a tour of the brewery and I'm pretty sure she couldn't travel too much. If I remember correctly... wait!" With a few keyboard strokes, Jon opens a page on the tablet and turns it so everyone can see. "It says here, 'the wife of Pearl Brewery president Otto Koehler, Emma put up with a lot, including her husband's brazen affairs. After Emma was injured in a car accident in 1910, Otto hired a nurse to care for her and ended up having an affair not just with the nurse, but also the nurse's best friend. Coincidentally, they were also named Emma, although the first nurse went by Emmi."

Eleanor set her pencil down. "Well, I'll be. He must have really liked the name Emma."

Bob snorted. "Or he just didn't want to make a mistake in the throes of passion and call out the wrong name."

Eleanor was visibly surprised. "I never thought of that. Some of you men can be scoundrels."

Jon held up a hand for everyone to get quiet. "It gets stranger. Otto eventually set up the two nurses in a house where he would visit them for their secret trysts. On one such visit, Nov. 12, 1914, Otto visited the house and some sort of argument occurred. The taller, blonde Emma shot him dead. She told police 'I'm sorry, but I had to kill him.' She was charged with murder, but fled to Europe to help as a WWI nurse. Four years later in 1916, Emma returned to and was found not guilty by an all-male jury. Later, she married one of the jurors."

Sandy took over the tablet and tried to find a picture of all three Emmas. She has pictures of her unknown woman from the box, and there are pictures of Emma Koehler, the owner of Pearl Brewery. They didn't match at all. "I'm trying to find pictures of the other Emmas, because my woman is definitely not Koehler. I love this story, but they seem to only have hair color in common."

Eleanor has now found her tablet and has it out and open. "Look here, it's a picture of the Emma who went to Europe after she killed Otto. She doesn't look like your girl, either. She's a blonde, too, and about the right age, but way too tall."

Jon had been reading on Sandy's tablet while she was checking out the photos of the two Emmas on Eleanor's tablet.

"What happened to the other nurse, Emmi?" Bill said.

Eleanor answered like they were on a scavenger hunt, "it says here she got married and wasn't heard from again."

Sandy, the ever-present researcher of strong Texas women starts, reading a passage from the Pearl Brewery website. "I wish I had learned about Emma Koehler earlier. She was one heck of a woman. Listen, 'Through all of this, Emma Koehler not only held her head high, but also went on to take over as CEO of the brewery after her husband's death and lead it to its most profitable years yet. During Prohibition, she pivoted to making 'near-beer', ice cream, and sodas and used part of the complex to run other businesses, like an auto repair shop and a dry cleaner. While breweries around her were shutting down, she was able to keep all her employees working. She relinquished control of Pearl in 1933, but stayed involved until she died in 1943.' Wow!"

Eleanor said, "That is so cool. Check this out, there is a hotel named after her, the Hotel Emma. You know, I'd like to stay there sometime. It says here that today, the vibrant Pearl Brewery complex is a hub for work, life and play in San Antonio, housing apartments, restaurants, shops, and even an outpost of the Culinary Institute of America. And at its center is the Hotel Emma, a stylish boutique property that tells guests the story of its strong-willed, business-savvy namesake."

Sandy wonders if her mystery woman is connected to the nurse, Emmi. That would be an extraordinary story. She was about to verbalize her thoughts when a dirty, dusty Fred enters the kitchen in a rush. Eleanor was the first to chastise him about the dust storm that blew in with him.

"Fred, what the devil are you doing? You're a mess. Get that filthy thing off this table. We eat here!"

Sandy and Jon have never heard Fred disagree with Eleanor ever, so when he just stopped and said, "No," the room went silent. The thing he has in his hands was dirty but you could see it was a fancy silk, drawstring bag of some sort. With the flourish of a magician, Fred pointed to the bag on the table and proceeded to tell his story while he opened the bag. "This bag was wedged in the wall upstairs where I was working. When I hit the wall for the third time, it dropped out. It's an amazing find!"

Sandy moved up close to see the treasure. The bag contained letters from an Emmi Larson of San Antonio, to an Emily McCormick of Twin Creeks, Texas. Everyone took a letter to read and all was quiet for a while. Jon was the first to shout "I got it!"

Everyone circled around. "Look, this is Emma, the one who killed Otto Koehler. This here is a picture of her and her husband. I think our mystery woman in the photo must be Emily."

Uncle Bob waved his letter. "Mine is another piece of the puzzle. It says she's excited to visit our Emma's hotel in Twin Creeks. This visit is to celebrate her sixty-fifth birthday. So, Emmi came to visit the other Emma, a.k.a. Emily McCormick. I think we found out who our mystery woman is."

Fred was so confused. "What are you talking about? Emma… Emmi… How do you know all that?"

Bill answered, "It all started with the Pearl Brewery Box. Then a little research and you brought the icing on the cake with the silk bag of letters." Fred was still confused so Eleanor shows him her tablet open to the story of Emma Koehler. He sat and read. Everyone else was still very carefully opening and reading letters. When Fred finished, "I think this discovery calls for a celebration.

Sandy agreed. Jon who had been searching on the other tablet looked up and said, "I have the perfect drink for this celebration. I am just not sure if we have all the right ingredients for it. It says here that the Hotel Emma was named after Emma Koehler before opening in November 2015. A drink called 'The Three Emmas' memorializes the women at the Sternewirth Bar inside the hotel. It's a drink made up of pearl beer, rose cordial, amontillado sherry, botanist gin, grapefruit, and lemon juice, according to the bar's menu. I think at the very least, we should have that drink at Sandy's grand opening."

Sandy pushed Jon aside to read the recipe herself and agreed. Her next thought was, would she like all those ingredients together? A trip to San Antonio to try one of theirs was in order. She had planned to go there to look for a suitable wedding gown anyway. Maybe she would stay at the Emma Hotel instead of the Menger Hotel, her personal favorite.

"So much excitement makes me hungry. Can we work on dinner? We've researched straight through lunch and halfway through the football games." Uncle Bob's comments has all the men turning on the big screen and settling in to watch traditional New Year's Day college football. Sandy, of course, is still with her tablet, copying and saving all the historical facts about the three Emmas. In her head, she realized she was beginning a new year and closing her last research for the women of her place.

Sandy liked watching football and Eleanor had shooed her away from the food preparations, so she sat down in front of her tablet again. Sandy didn't need to watch the TV screen every second because the men were not only watching every play, they were also breathing every play. So, when the air in the room was quiet and then followed by a burst of noise, she knew to look up and catch the replay.

Sandy decided that since her research on Emily,

a.k.a. Emma McCormick, met a dead-end, she would try to go backward. So, Maybelline McCormick was where she would start and work her way backward. Back in 2007 when she passed, there was lots of internet use but not out in rural Texas and certainly not at the hands of an elderly Maybelline. The courthouse here would be one of her stops to look at birth and death records.

Michael, Rosalie's grandson, had talked to his mom. Sandy had made arrangements to see her on January second. Sandy would see her tomorrow when she brought Rosalie to town to be at the front desk. Sandy was pretty sure all the commotion was over as far as Pete was concerned. Sandy still planned on having Rosalie at the front desk at the B&B whenever she could, and maybe two others working with her from the OHG group, plus Eleanor.

Eleanor turned to Sandy. "You know, Jane hasn't been allowed to come by because of the danger but since that has been tied up, I told George she could come by the last few days of Christmas break and help out if she wanted to."

Sandy snapped back to the present. "Yes, that would be nice. I have a meeting with Rosalie's daughter in the morning, so I won't be available for an hour or so around eight a.m."

Eleanor sat down next to Sandy. "Jane wants to do a presentation about one of the women of your rooms at school and asked if she could wear some of the clothing from the suitcase. I didn't think you would mind, so I washed all of them by hand and pressed them. Is that okay with you?"

Sandy remembered observing that Jane looked similar in size and shape to her girl in the picture. At that time, she saw her mysterious girl in everyone's face.

"Yes, that would be fun. We could take photos, then I could print them in black and white so the photos will look old and then she could put it in her report." Sandy's brain started to envision using the photos in her article by staging Jane, using the hotel as the backdrop. Jane holding her Emmas picture would be fun, too. Both young women were about the same age in the photo, give or take a year.

Jon moved away from the game and sat next to her. "Time for a break. Let's eat and then go watch the sun set. It's been a beautiful day and I am sure the sunset will be even better." Jon and Sandy set the table and everyone ate peacefully, except for cheering for touchdowns. Fred, Bob, and dad were still glued to the TV when Jon and Sandy stepped outside to sit on the porch, snuggled in a blanket wrapped in each other's arms. Tomorrow was one day closer to the trial.

FIFTEEN

THE NEXT MORNING STARTED EARLY and Sandy was ready. Jon went to the library to supervise the removal of all the equipment in his office. Sandy sat in the dining room waiting for Rosalie and her daughter. Eleanor had coffee and tea ready with some amazing cinnamon rolls from the Cynfully Delicious Bakery. "Sandy, I have a place setting for five because I'm sure Jane will arrive soon, too. I hope you don't mind?"

"Don't be silly Eleanor, that would be perfect. Jane needs to begin to enter the adult world of women. She could try on the clothes and model them for us so that we can see which fits her best. By the way, the last time Rosalie was here, she was telling me about Maybelline's last living relatives. Apparently, everything was all arranged for and they were driving down from Utah with their baby to inherit, but they never showed up and she passed not long after. Did you know anything about that?"

Before Eleanor can respond, Jane enters the front door with a gust of cold wind. "Hi everybody! It's so cold outside. Aunt Sue made me wear these ugly boots. She thinks they'll keep my feet warmer. I think tennis shoes are just fine. What's all the fancy dishes for?"

Before anyone could get an answer out, Rosalie and her daughter Elizabeth appeared in the doorway.

"Sandy? I'm Elizabeth Ballard, Michael's mom and Rosalie's daughter. You've really done a fantastic job on this B&B. It's lovely." Sandy and Elizabeth shake hands and head to the kitchen.

Eleanor had come to help Rosalie to a chair. Rosalie scolded her, "I can get around just fine. You do not have to babysit me. Hi there, Jane. Look at them boots you got on! I had a pair just like them when I was young."

"I bet you did. These seem like they're older than dirt. Aunt Sue says they were hers when she was young, like me. If they were cowboy boots, I might be okay but these lace-up shoes are just a pain to get in and out of."

Rosalie chuckled. "You're right, Jane, they were not meant to kick on and off easily. But they sure did keep your feet warm and dry."

Eleanor had disappeared and was back with several hangers full of clothes from the suitcase. "Jane, pick your favorite and try them on. Come show us when you get them on so we can take a few photos."

Sandy was up and showed Jane her favorite, and Rosalie and Elizabeth add their opinions to the mix. Jane headed out to change. Rosalie was very curious about the clothing. "Where did you get those? They seem to be the real deal."

Sandy explained about the things that she has found and Eleanor retrieved the boxes and the suitcase for Rosalie to look at. Rosalie thumbs through the belongings and looked up at Sandy. "This box belonged to Maybelline's mother, Emily. My understanding is that she was called Emma, short for Emily Mary McCormick, EMM."

Sandy was really listening; this was just the kind of information she wanted. Rosalie's memory was much clearer today. Rosalie started to talk through her memories. "I remember Maybelline talked about her mom being a woman of the world. She had worked as a lady's companion and nurse when needed, even though she had never been to school for it. Back in the day, schooling was not always needed if you had experience and good references. Maybelline's mom had traveled a lot for a girl of that time. She made it here to Twin Creeks when she was twenty-five and had Maybelline the first year she was here. She was kind of old to be having her first child at twenty-five, but never had any more live births after Maybelline."

Sandy was taking notes as Rosalie was telling her story and Eleanor had set her phone to record her words. Elizabeth, who had been quiet all this time, spoke. "My mom talks a lot about her friend and we talked about Maybelline these last few days. My mom is eighty-eight now and was seventy-five when Maybelline passed. Maybelline was eighty-one when she passed. I guess the court records can tell us when Emma, a.k.a. Emily passed. Mom thinks it was when she was fighting cancer and not around much. She doesn't have a memory of consoling Maybelline about her loss. She thinks they left town for the treatments."

Sandy held up the silk bag that Fred had found in the wall. "According to the letters we found in the wall, Emma's nurse friend from San Antonio, Emmi, was coming here to visit Emma for her sixty-fifth birthday. Rosalie, that would have made you thirty-four when Emmi came to visit Maybelline's mom. Do you remember?"

At that moment, Jane stepped back into the room. Rosalie gasped, "Oh my! How can you be here, Maybelline? Are you a ghost?"

Jane stopped dead and her mouth dropped open. Elizabeth glanced up and said, "My word, you are a spitting image of Maybelline, but mom, this is Jane. You know, the Guilroy's adopted daughter. Don't scare her with tales of ghosts."

Jane had paired one of the skirts that fell to the ankle and a lace blouse. She looked like she had just stepped out of a history picture book. Jane was so confused. "I look like who? I took out my pigtails and put it in a bun like your mystery lady, Sandy. I'm sorry if I did something wrong."

Eleanor had stood and had walked over next to Jane. "You've done nothing wrong. You look lovely. Rosalie thinks you look like an old friend of hers. It's okay."

Elizabeth decided that her mom needed to go home because Rosalie still was talking to

Jane like she was seeing Maybelline's ghost. Sandy asked Eleanor and Jane to meet her in the kitchen. Sandy helped Elizabeth with Rosalie to her car. "Elizabeth and Rosalie, I hope we can talk again soon." Both women nodded and drove away.

Sandy headed back to the kitchen. "Jane, you look amazing in that outfit. Let's take photos."

Eleanor held up her hand motioning to wait. "I have to add a little makeup to her before you snap those pictures."

Jane interrupts, "What happened? I mean, that little ol' lady has seen me before but never got crazy and called me a ghost. Whose ghost am I?"

"Let's get makeup on and photos taken, and then we will talk about ghosts. Okay?" said Sandy.

All agreed and the photoshoot began. Jane was a natural. Eleanor and Jane laughed and laughed at Sandy and her idea of historic photos. Sandy didn't care if they thought she was crazy, she knew this would go well in her article for the magazine. Eleanor took over. "Okay girls, I'm going to make lunch. Jane, you change. Sandy, once you get your camera stuff away, come to the kitchen. I should have lunch ready. We can talk there."

Ten minutes later, all three sat down to lunch and talk about Rosalie's ghost. Sandy had taken a moment to call Jane's aunt, Sue. Sue had decided to come by after Sandy explained the situation. Sandy said, "Eleanor, can we add another for lunch? Jane's aunt is joining us."

Eleanor was up and making another sandwich all the while talking. "Sue is coming here. That is so nice. I've been keeping her apprised of your progress here and she was wanting to come and peek at all the new décor."

The doorbell rang and Jane bounded for the door, sure it was her aunt, only to bring back Jon. A few seconds later, the bell rang again and this time it was Sue. Eleanor was now making a sandwich for Jon, too.

Jane was excited to share her experience. "Miss Rosalie thought I was a ghost."

Jon laughs. "Let's hear your best impression of this ghost. I can't wait."

Jane frowns at him but decides he isn't worth the time to scold so she did what teenagers do best… ignored him. Jane turned away from Jon and spoke, "To be exact, she thought I was her friend, the last owner of this place, Maybelline McCormick. Look at the pictures Sandy took of me in those clothes she found."

Jon is all into seeing the photos so he moves closer. "Wow, these are great! Sandy, are these what you were planning for your article or hotel brochure, or both?"

"Article? Brochure? Am I going to be in those!" Jane was back to excited and was hugging Sandy.

Jon realized he may have spilled the beans so he tried to backpedal. "I was just guessing…."

Sandy stopped him from making a fool of himself. "I would like to use some of these photos for both, but I haven't asked Sue or George for permission yet. I'm still in the planning period."

Sue hadn't said a word since they looked at the photos. She looked pale, kind of like she'd seen a ghost. Eleanor goes over close to Sue. "Sue, you okay? You look ill."

Sue looked up at Eleanor like she hadn't heard a word, so Eleanor repeated her question. Sue still didn't answer. She just stood up abruptly and began walking toward the door. "Oh look, a text message from George. Jane, we need to go... right now. Sorry everybody, but George needs both of us right now."

Sue motions for Jane to follow. They are out the door in seconds. Eleanor followed, but the front door shut before she got there. Sandy and Jon are right behind Eleanor. "I have known Sue for a long time. She can be a loner at times, but that was strange behavior even for her. I will call later and check on her."

"Jon, you almost had an angry teenager on your hands. Don't laugh at teenage girls unless she's laughing with you." Sandy was scolding Jon as the three of them went back to the kitchen to finish their sandwiches and clean-up.

Sandy was washing dishes when she asks, "Eleanor, I had a call from the high school wondering if we had a place for the new counselor, Zoe Long, until her new home is ready. She bought the old Ziegler place over by the high school but it's not going to be finished in time. Dad and Uncle Bob are in two of the rooms on the second-floor until after the trial. So, maybe the Happy Trails Room? I know it's the honeymoon suite but we don't have a newlywed couple wanting it. The third floor isn't complete yet and I don't want Fred trying to work around a guest."

Jon answers first, "Wow, the place is filling up. You have Rocky's friend, your dad, Uncle Bob, and now this counselor."

Eleanor finished drying the last dish. "I think Fred will be pleased you're not using the third floor until he finishes the plumbing. He knows that closing off the water to the third floor is essential, so it would be a problem if someone had to use it every day. So, I agree the Happy Trails Room is best. Wait maybe the Long room on the first floor. It has easy entry and exit from the back."

Sandy stopped to think. "I had earmarked that for Rocky's friend but I think you might be right. Let's do that, we can put Rocky's friend in the "Happy Trails room" if need be."

"Right after the trial, the new furniture will arrive. I decided to do it like this place would have been in the fifties. With the help of George and an estate sale we're going to in Dallas, I think there will be some really interesting treasures, I want one room to have a kind of western fifties vibe." Sandy stopped talking as the front doorbell alarm went off. Everyone picks up their phone to look at the camera, but Eleanor greets Bob and Sandy's dad returning from a quick trip to Dallas. They left early this morning and must have driven there and straight back. Sandy had expected them to stay overnight in Dallas.

Texans measure a trip in time, not miles, and this round trip was just three hours. Nothing big in Texas time.

"Hi dad. How was the drive?" Sandy greeted him with a hug and a kiss.

Bob answered first, "The trip was easy. The courthouse experience was a little weird. Some of Pete's associates were hanging around the courthouse. I guess waiting for you to appear. The agents there have decided that they will transport you, instead of all three of us, in one vehicle. Jon, do you mind going with Sandy? It would make both of us happier if she was not alone."

Jon nodded. "I had already planned on going, so this just makes it easier for me, too."

The men in her life were real men. She liked the independence she needed, but she also enjoyed the love and care she received from all three.

The streets around the courthouse in Dallas were busy. As Sandy looked out the darkened windows of the Suburban, she wondered out loud. "Where do you go in?" The driver answered by turning into an alley of sorts and stopped before an entrance. He and his partner said, "wait while we check things out." Sandy's nervous anxiety resurfaced. Could someone be waiting here for us? Jon was looking all around like he was feeling the stress, too. A few minutes passed, no gunfire or explosions, but Sandy still jumped closer to Jon when the door opened. The agent offered his hand and she hesitantly took it and slid out of the Suburban. The drop to the ground made Sandy a little unsteady on her feet, but the agent bent to steady her. At that moment, a shot pierced the window of the open door and would have killed the agent if he had been standing up straight. His instincts took over as he pulled Sandy in close and ran for the door a few feet away. Jon had his gun drawn and was returning fire to cover the run to the door. Just inside, other lawmen were passing them going out as they came running in. Jon stayed by the door to assist if needed.

Dad and Uncle Bob were already inside and came running to Jon and Sandy. "Are you two alright?" Both were visibly shaken. Sandy was just plain scared. "Is it safe in here?" Was all Sandy could get out. Two officers of the court ushered them into the bulletproof waiting area. Sandy watched through the glass as officials ran from front to back moving people to shelter. About ten minutes later, things seemed to settle down.

In this holding room for witnesses that might be in danger, the attendant was openly armed. Dad and Bob have concealed gun licenses like Sandy, but they were not armed. Jon, because of his former job, was allowed to carry. Thank goodness for that, because the man on the roof might have succeeded if Jon hadn't pinned him down with his returned fire.

Jon joined everyone in the holding room with some news. "The man on the roof was one of the few who did not get detained yesterday in the area sweep after Bob and your dad spotted them. It appears all is a go for the trial. You're up first, Sandy. What you say will determine who will and will not testify afterwards. This will probably take a while."

Jon's news was not welcome, but necessary to hear. He was right, Sandy was called about thirty minutes later. They ask her thousands of questions. Pete's lawyer was a pain in the neck and he was pushy. Pete kept looking at Sandy like she was in big trouble. She had seen that face before and it was usually followed by violence. Today, he shouted at her and the judge warned him to stop. The third time he was warned, he was silly enough to laugh at the judge and this judge had had enough. He moved him to a room where he could see and hear, but no one could see or hear him. This development made it easier to testify without his evil stares distracting Sandy. Finally, she was dismissed. She was exhausted. Jon must have been in the gallery listening because he arrived minutes after Sandy. Bob was missing when Sandy arrived and Dad said, "They just took Bob to testify about the beating he took. Then, I guess, maybe me."

Jon sat next to Sandy, "That's why I came back so quickly. It looks like my testimony and yours, Mr. McAllistor, are going to be used only if our story is disputed. So far, that has not happened. Bob's testimony is important because he was attacked like Sandy, so that allows for more years to be added to the sentence due to the seriousness of those attempts on their lives."

Sandy added, "Does that mean we can go

home?' Jon smiled, "Yes, we will go home tonight and will only come back if you're needed. With any luck, those attempts in Twin Creeks sealed his fate. At least, that's what Owen thinks."

Dad had been quiet, but when Bob appeared, he was up and asking questions. "So, Bob, how did it go?'

Bob was delighted to inform dad that Pete hadn't been in the courtroom, and instead had been put in the room for criminals who can't behave. "That was a pretty nice development, not having to look at him. It took me a minute to realize that he was moved in there. I guess it happened before I got in the room."

Sandy chimed in and gave a soft smile. "Oh, yea. That happened when I was on the stand. He kept disrupting court and then laughed at the judge when he was asked to be quiet. That pissed the judge off, so he warned him a final time. Then he went and said stupid stuff to the judge, so he had him moved in there."

Bob and dad laughed. "I guess he just can't contain himself. Nothing like cooking your own goose." Dad agreed with Bob. The door opened again and the clerk came in and dismissed them, telling them they could go on home.

Home had a nice ring to it, and even nicer so when there were family and friends waiting.

SIXTEEN

JANUARY IN TEXAS ALWAYS HAD unpredictable weather, from cold and wet, to pleasant and breezy. The days after the trial were nice, filled with visiting with dad and Uncle Bob. Jon seemed to fit in with the crew. Sitting out on the porch of the B&B had become one of Sandy's favorite things to do whenever she could. Dad and Uncle Bob left for Austin once they all got word the trial was over and they would not be needed again. Both Pete and Guy got long sentences. Sandy hoped that part of her world was gone. It felt good to be free.

After seeing her dad and Uncle Bob off, Sandy planned to spend a quiet moment reading on the front porch. It was a brisk, but dry day. The porch sheltered her from the prevailing wind especially when she went to the far end of the porch by the alley. To her surprise when she got there, her favorite chair was taken. Sitting in her chair was a sad-looking Jane.

"Hey Jane, how are you? I haven't seen you since the day Rosalie saw a ghost." With that introduction, Jane burst into tears. "Whoa,

whoa! What is going on?

"Something is wrong at home and I think I'm the one who did it but I don't know what I did."

Sandy squatted down in front of Jane and tried to calm her down. "Aren't you supposed to be at school?" More crying... Crap, that wasn't the thing to say. "School isn't that important today. You're more important. So, let's figure out what's wrong."

Jane blubbered out, "I'm what's wrong. I can't even say 'I'm sorry' cause I don't know what I did."

This part of the porch was close to the small window in the kitchen, so when the excited face of Eleanor came into view, Sandy was not surprised. She was, however, surprised when Jane's aunt Sue and uncle George came into view next. Seconds later, all three appeared on the porch and the commotion was too loud to stay outside. With a little coaxing by Eleanor, and the need for hot chocolate, everyone headed for the kitchen. To add to this commotion, the new counselor followed us in, just getting home from her day at school. Jon was sitting at the table reading, too. At least at some point, he had been reading. No one was doing any reading now with all of this commotion.

To Sandy's surprise, both George and Sue looked like they had been crying, too. What a mess.

Sandy decided this was her time to take charge. Jon stood as everyone entered. Eleanor went right to the stove where she already had water heating. Jon took Eleanor's lead and got out cups and saucers and cookies. Sandy began, "Okay, let's all sit here around the table and clear the air. It looks and sounds like a few questions need to be asked and answered. Sue, you and George sit here. Jane, sit across from them. Eleanor, you sit at the end close to the stove and Jon and I will sit at this end."

Just as everyone was seated Zoe, the counselor, came strolling into the kitchen with the brochure in her hand. "I love this brochure on Jane Long! I'm related to her." She stops dead, realizing she has stepped into a private meeting. "Ahhh… Sorry, I didn't mean to interrupt. I will ask about this later." Noticing Jane, she adds, "Hey, I think you're the young woman I was supposed to talk to this afternoon at school but I couldn't find you. Are you okay?"

That started Jane crying over again, which got everyone talking at once, again. This counselor knew that she had opened a can of worms, but she didn't even flinch. Zoe stood up taller and stuck her fingers in her mouth and let out an ear-piercing, coach-like whistle that stopped everyone dead in their tracks. "Hey everyone, settle. My comment about needing to talk to Jane was not to get anyone into trouble or upset. One of your teachers was worried about you and referred your name to me. I don't have a student load yet, so I went looking for you. We can talk at a later time." Zoe turned to leave when Sue stood and said, "Maybe you should stay. We might need your advice and then Jane would not have to miss any more class time."

Zoe saw Sandy give her the eyebrows up, universal signal shrug for, 'ok whatever works.' Zoe did not sit, she leaned against the counter looking like she was ready to bolt if need be.

Sandy started with Jane. "Jane, tell me what has you crying like this?"

Jane, who is still sobbing, tries to speak but a big hiccup comes out. She regains some composure. "I really don't know what I've done wrong but Aunt Sue and Uncle George have been arguing about me. I have never heard them argue like this before and it's scary. I don't like it."

Everyone, whether they were conscious of it or not, swiveled towards Sue and George. Sue bit her lip and George hung his head. After a pregnant pause, Sue began. "Jane, you have done nothing wrong. We're not angry with you. It is us that has a problem and we drug you into the middle. We are so sorry."

Jane frowns. "What have you drug me into? You are always so good to me, even when I do stupid things like skip school and hide here."

George slowly brought his head up. "We did a stupid but loving thing twelve years ago. We've been arguing about it because we don't know how to fix it now. We never thought it would come up after the first year or so. But here it is and we need to come clean. We don't want to hurt our most precious little girl."

Looking at the faces around the table, Jane was not the only one confused by his confession. Eleanor cleared her throat. "Can I help, Sue, by telling the story as you told me many years ago? It might be easier to hear it from a bystander that loves and cares for her, too."

Sandy and Jon were at a loss for words. Sue looked at George for guidance, he nodded. Sue turned to Eleanor. "Yes, that might work better than me sobbing through what needs to be said. Jane trusts you."

Fred had entered the room unseen and, sensing the seriousness of the situation, came and stood behind Eleanor as a show of support, putting his hands on her shoulders. Before Eleanor can start, he said, "If this had been Eleanor and my decision those many years ago, we would have done the same thing."

Eleanor looked up and smiled, then looked at everyone. "Please allow me to finish this story without interrupting. It will take all I have emotionally to do this. Sue and George are lifelong friends and I know how much they love you, Jane."

Jane was the only one who answered, "I want to know what's wrong. I'll do my best to be quiet."

Zoe leaned over Jane and put a tablet of paper and pen she found by the phone in front of Jane. "If you need to remember something, then write it down. It might help."

Jane looked up and smiled. "Thanks, they are teaching us that in communications class. Never thought I would have a real need for it. Okay, start your story, Eleanor."

Eleanor smiled a nervous smile. "Jane this

story is not my story, it's yours." Eleanor took a long sip of her drink and began, "about twelve years ago, Sue and George were on their way home after a long day of driving from a large estate auction near Lubbock. The weather was lovely. No storms, just big open sky with a ton of stars on a back-road shortcut, just west of Tolar. They came upon an accident, just one car. It was smoking. The car had run off the road and hit a tree. The driver was killed on impact. The tree was so big, it had pushed the engine in on the driver. Sue went to the back seat to retrieve the screaming baby in the car seat, while George went to get the woman in the front passenger seat out. She was badly injured. He did get her out and on to the ground. Sue called the police in Twin Creeks and they rerouted the call to a fire department closer to the accident, which sent an ambulance and fire truck to help."

Eleanor paused to take a sip of her drink, visibly steeling herself as she kept going.

"George was trying to stop the bleeding on the woman by applying pressure. He had to pry her hand away from a locket she was holding onto. The smoking vehicle at this time turned into a fire and Sue moved their car, with the baby in it, down the road so they would not be caught up in an explosion. The firetruck and paramedics passed Sue and George's car to get to the accident. The baby had gone to sleep by now. Sue rolled down the windows partially so she could hear the baby if she cried again, and then went back to the scene. George was kneeling over the woman when the paramedics arrived. The paramedics went to work on the woman. The locket was removed and handed to Sue as they tried to save the woman. The firemen attempted to put out the car fire while the paramedics loaded the woman onto a gurney to get her away from the burning car. The car was long gone and was impossible to contain the fire, then it exploded. Thank goodness everyone, including the woman, had been moved far away before it did. The policeman told George and Sue to go home, telling them he would be out to their place within the hour for a statement. George told the officer they would wait because they were tired and would likely sleep as soon as they got home. They had been driving for hours. He agreed, so they waited and answered all of his questions. George told the officer that if he thought of something else to ask, he worked at his dad's auction barn and to feel free to come by and ask. They got in the car and left."

Sandy could see where this was going, but when she looked at Jane's confused face, she could see Jane had not made the connection yet. Eleanor took another sip.

"So, when they got home it was 2:30 in the morning. They pulled in and Sue reached into the back seat for her purse and saw the baby and gasped. In all of the chaos and lack of sleep, they both had forgotten they still had the baby. Neither was in good enough shape to drive back, so they took the baby into their bedroom. George and Sue thought that the police would come by the next day. After a quick check on the baby, both laid down and went fast to sleep. Sue woke to the sound of a suckling noise and realized her hand that was dangling over the edge of the bed was being sucked by the most adorable creature she had ever laid eyes on and that this little girl needed food, and soon. Sue was up and working on that when George came into the kitchen. One thing leads to another and, three heavenly days later they still had not told anyone about the little girl and no one had come by to ask more questions. Sue had called around and learned that the mother, Sarah, had passed. Days turned into weeks, and then Sue heard more sad news from a distant cousin. She had lost her baby a few days after their home-birth. That baby, had she lived, would have been about the same age as their baby, Jane. With a little finagling of birth certificate paperwork, adoption papers, and some money handed over to the cousin, the baby could be officially theirs, at least in the eyes of the law. Sue and George had known for a long time that they couldn't have children, so this baby was sent to them from God and they would do their best to raise her right."

Sue, with tears running down her cheeks, pulled something from her pocket. "This locket, your locket, has a picture of your mom, dad and you. The other day... That picture you had taken... you were a spitting image of her."

Jane jumps up and inspects the locket. "It says 'My world. Sarah, Mitch and baby Jane.' That's me?" she breathes, her eyes filling with tears.

Sandy felt like her head had just lit up. When Jane read those names, she immediately recalled Rosalie telling her the names of Maybelline's last living relatives, Sarah and Mitchel Forester. Rather than sharing her own personal realization with the room, she decided she would bring it all up at a less emotional time.

Zoe stepped up close to Jane. "I think Sue and George must think a lot of your maturity to let you hear this story without any hesitation. I think they must trust you to understand and know how much they love you. If you look, you can see the sadness and the love in their faces. What a lucky girl you are."

Like magic, Sandy, Jon, Fred, Eleanor, and Zoe quietly left the kitchen for the library. This little family needed a minute of privacy. A few quiet moments later, Sue, George and Jane appeared in the doorway to the library said their goodbyes and left.

Zoe stood to leave, then turned back. "You know, I'm legally obligated to do something about this. The law is clear, but the most important part of that law is doing what is in the best interest of the child. I think Jane's best interest is to be with those lovely, caring parents for now."

Everyone nodded and Zoe headed towards the kitchen and back to her room. Eleanor and Fred excused themselves to the kitchen.

Jon turned to Sandy. "Could this get any crazier? Let's find a quiet place to be. I have some research and we need to make reservations."

Sandy nodded then grabbed his hand. "I'm sure Jane will be okay. Sue and George treasure her. Let's get us together."

Sandy's new world rotated around Jon and the B&B, and Sandy liked that idea. Jon and Sandy had thought about a road trip to San Antonio. First, to look at wedding dresses and visit the Emma Hotel in San Antonio. They would stop and check on Uncle Bob on the way. Valentine's Day seemed to be the perfect time. Jane's crazy development, and Sandy's new discovery, would just have to wait for a day or two. Jane was in the good hands of Sue and George, with Eleanor, Fred, and Zoe around to help.

Today, Sandy was ready for her plans to be all about herself and Jon.

Read more of Jane's story in Book 2 of this series.

ABOUT THE AUTHOR

Cathy O'Bryan is an author with 30 years experience in teaching Theatre, Art, and Competitive Speech and Debate. Her first two novels "A Child of the Cold War Code Name Kitten" and "Growing up in the Cold War Code Name Kitten" have been very fulfilling and have received great reviews.

With this novel she has entered an interesting collaboration with several other authors to work on a series of books in "Twin Creeks, Texas." This first novel in the series of her four was inspired by three talented authors who welcomed her into their fold. Following this book "Taken for

Granite" by Robin B.Sweet should be published in less than a month. Cathy's second book in this series should be ready for Christmas 2020 with more to come.

Happy reading!